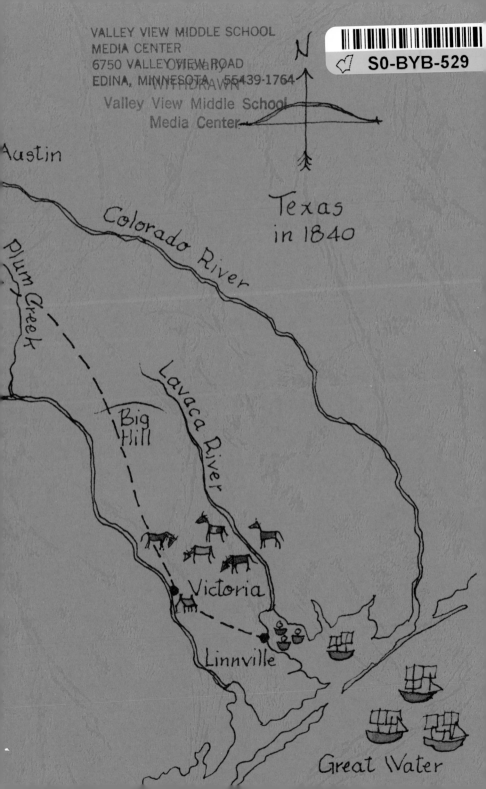

S0-BYB-529

N

Austin

Colorado River

Plum Creek

Lavaca River

Big Hill

Texas
in 1840

Victoria

Linnville

Great Water

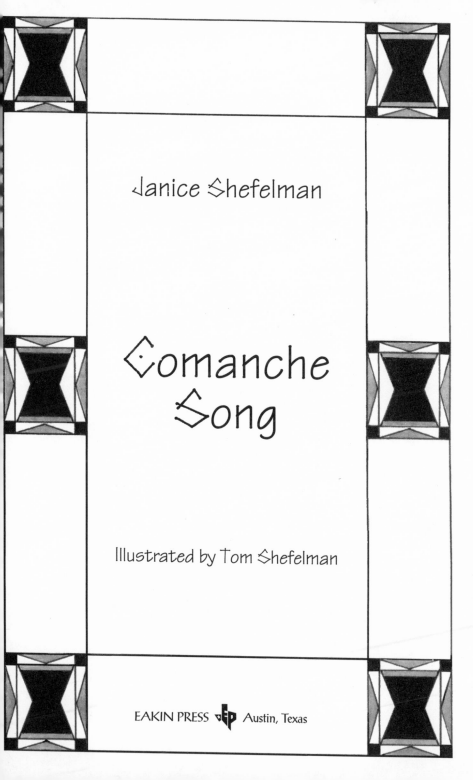

Janice Shefelman

Comanche Song

Illustrated by Tom Shefelman

EAKIN PRESS Austin, Texas

Edited by Melissa Roberts
Designed by Virginia Messer
Pat Molenaar
and the Shefelmans

Library of Congress Cataloging-in-Publication Data

Shefelman, Janice Jordan
Comanche song / by Janice Shefelman;
illustrated by Tom Shefelman.
p.   cm.
Summary: A young Comanche boy experiences
his tribe's conflicts with the Tejanos in 1840s Texas.
ISBN 1-57168-397-6
1. Comanche Indians—Juvenile fiction. [1. Comanche Indians—Fiction.
2. Indians of North America—Texas—Fiction.]
I. Shefelman, Tom, ill.   II. Title.
PZ7.S54115 Co 2000
[Fic]—dc21
00-025328

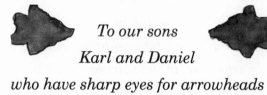

To our sons
Karl and Daniel
who have sharp eyes for arrowheads

Their arrows are broken and their springs are dried up...
Their council fires have long since gone out...
and their war cry is fast dying away...
They will live only in the songs
and chronicles of their exterminators.
Let these be true to their rude virtues as men,
and pay tribute to their unhappy fate as a people.

—Charles Sprague
from *Comanches*
by T. R. Fehrenbach

Contents

Names of Characters

Since Comanches did not have a written language, white men spelled their names phonetically in various ways. Pronunciation is the reader's choice.

Tsena's Village

AHSENAP—*Tsena's grandfather*
CHAWAKEH—*Tsena's little sister*
EKAKURA—*one of Quasia's wives; Kiyou's mother*
ISIMANICA—*war chief; Kiyou's uncle*
KIANCETA—*Tsena's best friend*
KIYOU—*Tsena's half-brother*
QUASIA—*peace chief; Tsena's father*
SEMANAW—*Tsena's grandmother*
TOPAY—*Tsena's mother*
TSENA—*son of the peace chief*
YUANEH—*Tsena's mare*

Muguara's Village

ANAWAKEO—*Chief Muguara's granddaughter*
COTOPA—*aide to Chief Muguara*
MOKO—*Chief Muguara's wife; grandmother of Anawakeo*
MUGUARA—*chief of the Twelve Bands*

Other Villages

NAPAWAT—*old blind warrior*
PIAVA—*war chief who comes to parley*
POCHANA QUOHEEP—*war chief who takes Muguara's place*

Texas Army Officials

COLONEL COOKE—*senior officer in the council house*
COLONEL FISHER—*officer in charge of troops at San José*
CAPTAIN HOWARD—*officer in charge of parley with Piava*
CAPTAIN REDD—*officer who befriends Tsena*

Smithers Household

CARMENCITA—*a servant*
SEÑOR PECK—*teacher of Will and Agatha*
AGATHA SMITHERS—*Will's little sister*
DOCTOR SMITHERS—*Will's father*
SEÑORA SMITHERS—*Will's mother*
WILL SMITHERS—*the boy who finds Tsena*

Author's Note

Comanches called themselves *Nemena,* which means "the People" or "the True Human Beings." From the high plains to the hill country of Texas they hunted, warred, loved, raised children, and treated Mother Earth with reverence. Then came white man, who took their land and destroyed their way of life.

Comanche Song is based on two historical encounters between the Penateka Comanches and Texans in 1840: the Council House Massacre and the Battle of Plum Creek. I chose to see these events through the eyes of a Comanche boy. Although Tsena and his family are fictional, some of the characters are historical: Chief Muguara and Pochana Quoheep (called Buffalo Hump by Texans) were well-known chiefs of the time. And the beautiful red-haired captive who read aloud to the Comanches was Juliet Watts. She survived the battle that ensued.

All the places in the story are real. The creek that runs by Tsena's village is on my family's ranch near Mason, Texas, where we have found many Comanche arrowheads and climbed Lone Hill.

1

War Drill

It was white man's year of 1840. Tsena ducked out of his lodge and stood looking across the ravine to the hills beyond. He could not know that it was also the year white man would change his life forever. No one in the village could know.

He shivered in the cold, clear air and lifted his arms to the first rays of the rising sun. "Father Sun, let your power enter my body so that I can become a great warrior."

Down by the creek his red mare raised her head and looked at him. Tsena always kept Yuaneh beside the lodge at night, tied to his wrist, but at first light he untied her. Cupping his hands around his mouth he made the call of a hawk, "*Haw, haw, haw.*" Yuaneh came trotting up the slope to him, water still dripping from her muzzle.

"Time for the war drill, my little mare." Tsena stroked the white blaze on her forehead. "The war chief will be watching us today, but it is nothing to worry about."

Yuaneh's ears turned to catch his words.

"Just pretend this is one of our practices." Tsena pulled on the loop of rope braided into her golden mane. *Good*, he thought, *it is tight.* He would need it to hold him when he clung to her side.

He leaped onto her back, and Yuaneh pranced through the village. Women were already at work scraping hides. One after another glanced up and smiled at him. He could feel their eyes on him after he went by.

"A fine young man," said one. "So polite—like his father."

"Yes," said another, "he is beginning to look more and more like his father—same lean face and body. Perhaps he will make a peace chief too."

Tsena hurried on. Little did they know what he thought. In fact, even *he* did not know what he thought. Sometimes he wanted to be peace chief like his father, but other times he wanted to be war chief like Isimanica. He felt pulled in two directions, as the string is pulled from the bow. But one thing he did know—first he had to prove himself on the warpath. And before going on the warpath he had to seek his vision and find a guardian spirit.

Out in the meadow boys had begun to gather. His half-brother Kiyou was there, mounted on his paint. *If he lets his tongue flap this morning . . .*, thought Tsena as he clenched his fists.

No sooner did he have the thought than Kiyou yelled, "Hey Grandfather, isn't it time to go to council with the old men?"

Tsena rode up to Kiyou, stopped, and looked at him for a moment, his fists still clenched. "Words fall out of your mouth like coyote droppings, Kiyou."

A few boys laughed.

"*Och*, it is Chief Fancy Tongue instead," Kiyou said. "Too bad you cannot fight like you talk."

Tsena thought of his grandfather's words: *It is not manly to fight among ourselves.* He unclenched his fists and said, "If only you could think before you talk."

Kiyou moved his horse closer and gave Tsena a shove.

"Do not do that again," Tsena said.

"What if I do?" Kiyou reached out and shoved him harder.

Tsena grabbed his arm and felt himself being pulled off Yuaneh, onto the ground. They rolled over and over. All the boys gathered around, shouting. For a moment Tsena was on top.

"Come on, Tsena, show him." It was Kianceta.

Then, grunting, Kiyou heaved himself up and pinned Tsena's shoulders with his muscular arms.

"Yes, show me, Fancy Tongue," Kiyou said and thrust his leering face closer.

Tsena heaved his body this way and that, but Kiyou was like a rock.

Suddenly, the shouting stopped, and the boys made way for the hulking form that strode into the circle. Chief Isimanica. With his feet planted wide apart and his arms folded across his chest, he stared at them.

For a moment the two boys froze. Then Kiyou got off and stood, and Tsena scrambled up beside him.

The war chief was a powerful man with full lips and narrow slit-eyes that seemed to take in everything and reveal nothing.

"Forgive me, Uncle," said Kiyou.

Isimanica nodded and looked at Tsena.

"I know it is not manly to fight among ourselves, Chief Isimanica. I am shamed."

Isimanica frowned. "Just show that kind of fury against the enemy and you will make good warriors—both of you." He paused, his eyes sliding from one boy to the other. "However, I did not come to watch you fight this morning. I came to see if you are ready for the warpath." He let his eyes slide around the circle of boys.

"There are those in our village who would have the *Nemena* grow weak and not go on the warpath."

Tsena shifted uneasily. Everyone knew the chief was talking about his father.

"But I say, if we don't make war, the *tejanos* will build their lodges on land the Great Spirit gave to us for hunting. The only way to keep them off is to take the warpath."

The words fired Tsena's blood. He would show Isimanica that he was ready.

"So, enough talk," the chief said. "Words come easily, but not the skills of war." He walked alone out to the dummy that lay like a wounded warrior in the meadow and picked it up. Stuffed with sand and straw, it weighed as much as a small man. The boys had named the dummy Pahtooeh.

Isimanica let the dummy drop and returned. "So, young warriors, you already know that your first duty is to rescue a fallen comrade. Now show me how you do that."

The boys mounted and rode silently to the far end of the meadow, with Kiyou leading the way. *One thing is certain*, Tsena thought, *if Kiyou ever falls off his horse, he can just lie there.*

The war chief motioned for someone to come.

Kiyou slipped the loop over his head and gave his horse the quirt. The paint bolted into a gallop. At the last moment Kiyou reached down, grabbed Pahtooeh, and flung him across his horse.

Oh, he is good, thought Tsena.

Kianceta took his turn next, "to get it over with," he said. When he tried to pick up the dummy his horse shied, and Pahtooeh fell from his hands.

One by one the boys rode out. Two of the younger ones dragged the poor dummy beside them. If Pahtooeh were a real man he would not have much skin left. Still, it was better than being scalped by the enemy.

Then it was Tsena's turn. He stroked Yuaneh's neck. "Just do what you always do." Putting an arm through the loop and pulling it over his head, he nudged the mare with his heels.

As they galloped toward the dummy, Tsena leaned into the loop, his left foot hooked over Yuaneh's back, his right curled under her belly. Yuaneh's hooves pounded beside his head. He kept his eyes on the dummy. Reaching out, Tsena grasped him. With one heave that seemed to tear his arms from their sockets, he flung the dummy across Yuaneh.

For a moment Tsena lay over the dummy, breathing hard as his mare turned. Then he leaned back and shouted, "We did it, Yuaneh . . . thank the spirits!" He dropped the dummy in the center of the meadow and joined the others.

When all the boys had dismounted and gathered around, Isimanica said, "I am pleased by what I see. Most of you performed like young warriors."

Tsena's heart swelled for he felt sure he was one of the "most."

The chief looked first at Kiyou. "You, Nephew, showed great skill and strength for so young a warrior."

"Thank you, Uncle. It is because of your lessons." Kiyou raised his chin and shot a look at Tsena.

Then to Kianceta the chief said, "You have to show your horse who is master."

Kianceta nodded with his eyes cast down.

As Isimanica commented on each boy's ride, Tsena began to wonder if he had been forgotten.

Last of all Isimanica fixed his eyes on Tsena. Those eyes made him uneasy. He could not tell what the chief was thinking. Had he, Tsena, done something wrong? Then a little smile spread Isimanica's lips. "For a son of the peace chief, you did not do so badly," he said.

Not so badly! Tsena had hoped for more, yearned for real praise from the war chief. *It is all because of Father*, he thought. Still, he nodded his thanks.

Isimanica looked at the sun, which had risen half-way up the sky, warming the air. "That is all for today. Tomorrow I will watch your mounted target practice." Then he turned and strode toward the village.

For the first time Tsena saw that Grandfather Ahsenap was sitting at the edge of the meadow, watching. Had he been there long enough to see the fight?

Ahsenap motioned for Tsena to come. With Yuaneh following, he walked over and sat down beside his grandfather. At first he could not look at him for fear of seeing disapproval in his face.

"I am proud, Grandson," he said in his gritty voice. "You handle your horse with much skill."

Surprised, Tsena looked up. "Thank you, Grandfather."

Although Ahsenap's right eyelid drooped nearly shut, his left eye was sharp, and in it there was a spark of amusement. Tsena waited for him to go on.

"He who controls his horse makes a good warrior," his grandfather said, "but he who controls himself makes a good leader."

Tsena looked down at the ground again. His grandfather had seen the fight.

"You will learn," Ahsenap said quietly, "because you listen well—and I am a good teacher." He smiled, showing his straggly teeth.

Ever since Tsena could remember, his grandfather had taken him to council meetings. When he was a small boy he sat between the old man's folded legs and listened to council talk. If Tsena became restless, Ahsenap put his hands on the boy's shoulders to calm him. He needed to hear how men spoke in council, his grandfather said, so that one day he could take his father's place.

But now Ahsenap was so old, so painfully old. Leaning on one arm he grunted and pushed himself up. Tsena stood too, towering over him. It made his heart ache to see his grandfather bent under the weight of his years. *He will not always be here*, thought Tsena, *and the world will seem empty without him.*

All at once the dogs began to bark and run toward the ravine. Women stopped their work as men came out of their lodges with bows in hand. The old men left their dice on the ground and turned to look.

"I'll go and see who comes," Tsena said. He darted between lodges, past racks of drying meat, leaped over a hide staked to the ground, and made his way through the gathering crowd to stand at the edge of the ravine beside his father, Quasia.

On the other side a mounted warrior raised his arm in greeting.

A Visitor

He was one of the *Nemena*. Tsena could see that by the long fringe on his leggings and moccasins. But *who* was he and what news did he bring?

The dogs stopped barking and trotted to the visitor as he started down the slope. They could smell the difference between friend and enemy.

"Do you know him, Father?" Tsena asked.

"It is Cotopa, Chief Muguara's aide," said Quasia. Then, turning to Tsena's mother, he said, "Go, Topay, and prepare food for our guest."

She nodded and slipped away through the crowd.

Tsena knew who Chief Muguara was. Everyone knew. If he sent his aide here it must be important,

Tsena realized, for he was the most powerful chief of the Twelve Bands.

Tsena kept his eyes fixed on Cotopa. The young warrior held himself erect, his head thrown back, obviously proud to be the great chief's aide. What message was he bringing?

He rode up the slope and dismounted in front of Quasia.

"Welcome to our village, Cotopa," said Quasia, grasping him by the shoulders. They touched their cheeks together, first one side and then the other.

"Thank you, Chief Quasia. I bring news from Chief Muguara that will make your heart glad. He has had a vision. He feels that the omens are good now for seeking peace with the *tejanos*."

Peace? Tsena wondered. *Chief Muguara?* It did not sound like him.

A slow smile spread across Quasia's face. "That is good news, Cotopa. I will call for a council. But first you must have something to eat." He put his hand on Tsena's shoulder. "My son Tsena will take care of your horse."

Cotopa turned to him, nodding his thanks.

"Come to council with your grandfather," Quasia told Tsena. "I want you to hear Chief Muguara's vision."

"I will, Father."

Tsena walked Cotopa's horse down to the creek. Meanwhile the women went back to their work, the boys back to practicing on their own, and children back to their play. Tsena stood thinking as the horse drank his fill. *Even if the* tejanos *promise to stay off our land, what does it mean? They have forked tongues. They have broken treaties before—they will break them again. The only white men who keep treaties are the* Alemanes, *not the* tejanos.

When he saw that the councilors were gathering at his father's lodge, Tsena led the horse up the slope to the meadow and tethered him. Then he hurried to stand beside his grandfather and the other councilors waiting outside. Ahsenap nodded his approval but looked away and said nothing. He seemed to be considering the words he would speak, so Tsena kept his silence too.

After a time Quasia stepped out of the opening. "We are ready now . . . please come in."

Following Ahsenap to his usual place in the circle, Tsena sat down behind him. He looked around at the men. Quasia took his place facing the doorway next to Cotopa. Across the circle sat Isimanica. *As it should be*, Tsena thought. *They sit on opposite sides of the fire as they are on opposite sides of the* tejano *problem*. In the center a handful of grass smoldered, sending up smoke and filling the lodge with its sweet odor. But pleasing though it was, it did not mask the tension between Quasia and the war chief.

Quasia held up the sacred pipe in both hands, letting the feathers dangle. Then he put it to his lips, inhaled, and blew the first puff of smoke up to the Great Spirit, the next down to Mother Earth, and then to the four directions.

He passed the pipe to Cotopa, who smoked and passed it on. One by one each man in the circle smoked. Tsena watched, imagining the day when he would become a man and could smoke the pipe and feel the breath of the Great Spirit inside his body.

After Quasia cleaned the pipe and placed it on the robe before him, he nodded to Cotopa.

Cotopa arose, composed himself, and began. "Esteemed councilors, two sleeps ago Chief Muguara had a vision. He saw white horses galloping across the prairie." Cotopa raised his arm and looked into some place beyond the lodge, as if he could see the horses. "When they came to the Great Scarp, they clambered up to higher land, where a herd of buffalo grazed.

"The buffalo chief lifted his huge head and bellowed, 'Go back to the south where you came from. This is our grazing ground.'

"The horse chief came forward and said, 'O, Chief of the Buffalo, if you promise to stay north of the Great Scarp, we will keep to the south as long as the rivers flow.'

"And so the buffalo and the horses agreed that the Great Scarp was a line between them."

Cotopa paused and folded his arms across his chest. "Chief Muguara sends his vision to you as a sign that the time has come to treat with the *tejanos*. He calls for a tribal council three sleeps from now. That is all." With those words Cotopa sat down.

Tsena marveled at the vision. It seemed almost too perfect. Did Chief Muguara make it up? He had a reputation as a wise and wily old chief.

Quasia unfolded his legs and stood, seemingly without effort. Everyone grew still. For a moment he focused his gaze above the circle. He was a tall, sinewy man. Looking up at him, Tsena was filled with pride to be his son.

"Chief Muguara is wise," Quasia began. "He understands that our differences with the *tejanos* can no longer be settled by war."

He looked directly at Isimanica for a moment. Isimanica returned his look, his mouth shut in a thin, hard line that turned down at the corners. *There is going to be trouble*, Tsena said to himself.

"The *tejanos* can afford to lose many warriors," Quasia went on. "They are as numerous as the blades of grass, while our numbers shrink even as the snow melts on a warm day." He paused, letting his words hang in the air. No one stirred. They were eloquent words, but eloquence had never impressed Isimanica.

"So, my fellow councilors," he went on, "let us agree on a line between us and make peace."

As Quasia sat down, the councilors began to shift about, speaking quietly among themselves. Tsena sat rigid, his eyes fixed on Isimanica. The war chief gathered himself up and stood. He took a wide stance and folded his arms across his chest. The councilors fell silent.

"The *tejanos* will stop at no such line. They may sign a treaty, but they are faithless. They break treaties as easily as breaking a twig." Isimanica frowned. "No, the *only* way to show them the land is ours is to kill any man who steps upon it!"

Tsena felt his heart begin to beat a little faster.

Isimanica pushed up the sleeve of his buckskin shirt, showing a tattoo around a scar. "Here a *tejano* bullet spilled my blood. But before he could reload I drove my spear into his heart." He raised his chin. "Never will that *tejano* build his lodge on our hunting grounds. And never will I go to them on my knees to beg for land that is already ours. I go instead to war." His eyes blazed as he looked around the circle and sat down.

By this time Tsena's heart was racing. He was ready to follow Isimanica on the warpath.

Then Ahsenap stood on his old bowed legs.

"We have a saying among our people that the brave die young. But I say, the wise grow old." The corner of his mouth twitched, and he paused.

"When the young stop listening to the elders, they run blindly like buffalo and follow one another over the cliff to die." He turned to look briefly at Tsena with his one good eye. "So listen well. White men are human like us. They love their children and they would rather live than die even as we would. I say, we can both live here without killing the other." He sat down and folded his legs.

It seemed to Tsena that he had no mind of his own—the bow and the string again. He could listen to Isimanica and believe him and then listen to his grandfather and believe him. Was his grandfather wiser than Isimanica because he had lived for sixty-four winters? Or did Ahsenap want peace because he could no longer go on the warpath?

Old Tekwitchi stood with the help of a cane and said, "If there are so many *tejanos* as Quasia says, we had better deal with them peacefully, for we can no more stop them than we can stop the sun from rising."

Mumserku, the *puhakut*, spoke next. "Visions to make war come often, but visions to make peace come rarely. Why not treat with the *tejanos*? If they speak with a forked tongue, then we will go on the warpath." He looked at Isimanica for a sign of agreement, but the war chief gave none.

To Tsena these words seemed wisest of all.

After everyone who wished to had spoken, only Isimanica was opposed to the idea of making a treaty. Quasia stood once more and looked around the circle.

"I propose to go to Chief Muguara's village and speak with the other chiefs. What is the will of the council?"

Each councilor answered in turn with a nod. Then the war chief stood.

"I will have nothing to do with a treaty." His sliding eyes flashed. "I am not what white man calls a *good* Indian—a good Indian gets nothing but trinkets. A *bad* Indian is one who keeps the land he roams, because no white man dares step onto it."

He looked directly at Quasia. "But I would not want to keep our peace chief from making a fool of himself. Perhaps he prefers trinkets to land." He stalked to the doorway, flung back the flap, and was gone.

Tsena caught his breath. Such behavior was unheard of in council. There was a stunned silence. Quasia remained standing, his face expressionless. He seemed to be waiting until those words were caught up in the column of smoke rising out of the smoke hole.

At last he spoke in a low voice. "Then the council is unanimous. Let the crier go and shout the news that all may hear. I leave tomorrow for Chief Muguara's village, and I take my son Tsena with me." He lifted his chin. "We shall see who is the fool."

A Journey

Tsena woke up once during the night. On the other side of the fire pit his sister Chawakeh was a small lump under her buffalo robe. His mother's bed was empty. With Father, Tsena guessed, for he called her to his lodge more often than he called his other two wives.

Tsena was still awake when she returned, but he pretended to be asleep. Topay paused beside him, reached down, and touched his cheek.

Did she not know he was nearly a man now, too old to be mothered? And yet, there were times when he wished he could be a little boy again, safely running around the village on his stick horse. Och, *if Kiyou knew that, would he not laugh!* Tsena thought.

After his mother had gone to bed, he rolled over on his back and looked up at the stars through the smoke hole. He was sixteen winters old. Soon he would go on the warpath, and that both excited and frightened him. *Yes*, he thought, *I must ask Father again to speak to the* puhakut *about my vision quest. If I had a guardian spirit, maybe I would not be afraid.*

The stars were beginning to fade in the first light of day when Tsena awoke again. His heart gave a little leap. For now, at least, he did not have to worry about the warpath. He was going on the peace path today, to Chief Muguara's village, where all the great chiefs of the Twelve Bands would gather.

Topay and Chawakeh were still asleep. Tsena untied the rope around his wrist and picked up the dress clothes that his mother had laid out for him. Opening the door flap, he stepped outside.

Yuaneh nuzzled him as he undid her hobble, and together they walked down to the men's bathing pool. While Yuaneh drank, Tsena plunged into the icy water. It snatched the breath from his throat and set his heart racing.

Hurriedly he washed, climbed out, and brushed the water from his body. Only after he slipped into his shirt and leggings could he draw a deep breath. He swung his shoulders back and forth to make the beaded fringe sway. The clothes made him feel like one of the chiefs.

As he and Yuaneh started back to the village, Chawakeh came skipping down the slope. At her heels ran her furry black puppy. She glanced at Tsena, but quickly looked away. She was becoming shy with him now that he was nearly a man. It was proper for her to do so, but it saddened him. Everything was changing so fast.

He opened the door flap and ducked inside the lodge. His mother knelt at the fire, roasting venison.

"Good morning, my son," she said. "How fine you look."

"Thank you, Mother." He sat down on a robe and watched her cook. She had painted a circle of red on her cheeks, a red stripe along the part in her hair, and she wore her best doeskin dress. *For Father's leaving*, he thought. He marveled at how she adored him. *Will I ever find a girl who adores me like that?*

In a moment Quasia pulled aside the door flap, stepped in, and stood looking down at them.

"You honor me, my husband," Topay said with a teasing lilt in her voice. She placed the venison on a stone and began slicing it.

"I come because you are the best cook among my wives," Quasia said. The corners of his mouth twitched as he settled himself.

Tsena loved the playfulness between them. Topay knew very well that he came because she was his favorite wife.

Chawakeh stepped through the doorway, set the water bag down, and flung her arms around Quasia's neck.

"Good morning, my little prairie flower!" Quasia greeted her.

The puppy jumped about them, putting his paws on Chawakeh's back.

"Down, Ona!" she said. The puppy obediently lay down by the fire and looked up at her. Turning back to her father, Chawakeh fingered the silver pendants on his breastplate. "You are all dressed up, Father."

"Yes, little flower, for the tribal council."

"Can I go too?" she asked.

"You know better than that, my daughter," said Topay.

While Chawakeh pouted, Topay served the venison onto small hides and handed them around. There was honey sauce for dipping and a bowl of dried figs and persimmons.

Quasia offered a morsel to the Great Spirit, and then placed it in the fire. They ate silently for a while. Tsena felt his father's eyes on him. What was he thinking? Sometimes Tsena wished his father could be playful with him like he was with Topay and Chawakeh.

At last Quasia said, "Our son is no longer a child, Topay." He seemed to be realizing it for the first time. "His legs outgrow his body."

Tsena looked up at him. This was the time to ask. "No, Father, I am not a child anymore. It is time for me

31

to seek my vision. Will you speak to the *puhakut* when we return?"

Quasia looked back at the fire. The words hung in the air between them. It was not the first time Tsena had asked. Before, his father had said only that he was too young.

Topay watched Quasia from the corners of her eyes, while Chawakeh slipped a bite of meat to Ona.

"There is no hurry for you to become a warrior, my son," he said then. "That will happen soon enough. And with a war chief like Isimanica, you would be off on a senseless warpath."

"How else am I to bring honor to myself, Father?"

"You have already done so on the hunt."

"But that is not enough," Tsena said. "I have to show that I am a brave warrior."

"There are other ways." Quasia smiled and put a hand on Tsena's shoulder. "Be patient, my son. As soon as we have a chance to treat with the *tejanos*, I will speak to Mumserku."

So, at last Tsena had a promise, even though he did not understand what "other ways" there could be. Quasia himself had gone on the warpath and proved his bravery, though he was proud of the fact that he had never killed a man. He went on the warpath only to take horses, and he had taken many.

After breakfast they made themselves ready. Tsena mixed red powder and oil in a bowl and painted stripes across his cheeks. Topay knelt behind Quasia and braided his long hair and wrapped the braids in rabbit fur. Then she braided his scalp lock and stuck his eagle feather in it. Next she did Tsena's hair while Quasia painted his face. As she tugged gently on his braids, Tsena fingered the small beaded bag that hung around his neck, his medicine bag. One day soon it would hold his vision objects. What would they be? What would his vision be?

And then it was time to leave. Chawakeh had been watching Quasia paint his face. Suddenly, she stuck her finger in the bowl and smeared a red mark on her cheek.

"See, Father," she said, "I can come too!"

Quasia laughed and picked her up as he stood. In spite of the fact that she was six winters old, he swung her over his head.

"No, my prairie flower, you must stay here and take care of your mother while I am gone."

When he set her down again Chawakeh nodded, but tears welled in her eyes.

"And you, my son," Topay said, "take care of your father." Her eyes flashed with fun. "Don't let him lose his way home."

They all laughed—even Chawakeh, as her tears made the red paint run.

Quasia clasped Topay in his arms for a moment, then turned and stepped outside. Tsena picked up his bowcase and followed.

People had gathered to bid them farewell. Quasia's

other two wives, Puki and Ekakura, Kiyou's mother, were there. Kiyou was already out in the meadow with the boys.

Ekakura came to Quasia. She was a tall, proud-looking woman. "Our son wishes me to say farewell. As you see," she said, gesturing toward the meadow, "he practices to bring honor to his family."

Quasia looked at her for a moment without speaking. Then he said, "Kiyou has my seed, Ekakura, but he has the heart of your brother."

She stepped back as if struck by his words. Quasia was talking about Isimanica.

Quasia softened his tone. "It is true we need strong warriors. But we also need peacemakers."

Is that what Father meant? Tsena wondered. *He wants me to be a peacemaker. Will that bring honor or ridicule?*

Ahsenap came and took Tsena's hand in his rough ones. "Listen well to the words you hear in the council lodge, Grandson."

Tsena grinned. Ahsenap saw his thoughts, even if he had only one good eye.

Then he said farewell to Grandmother Semanaw. She was a small woman, but she held her chin high so that she seemed to look down on people. Tsena had always been a little afraid of her, yet he knew she loved him.

"See that you bear yourself in the manner of a great chief's son," she said.

Tsena nodded. "I will, Grandmother."

Quasia, Cotopa, and Tsena mounted their horses and started down the slope.

"Farewell, Tsena," Kianceta called, running up at the last moment.

"Farewell, Ceta. Take care of Pahtooeh while I am gone."

Kianceta nodded, grinning.

They rode across the creek and up to the top of the ravine. Tsena raised his arm in one last farewell. Then he turned and looked across the valley, past Lone Hill to the blue hills beyond. The sun had risen three fingers above the horizon, and they headed just south of it. He felt like an arrow that flies across the sky to some unknown place.

For a while they rode without talking—Tsena following his father and Cotopa. Yuaneh frisked about, glad to be starting off. Tsena patted her neck. "Yes, Yuaneh, I feel the same way."

As they passed by Lone Hill, its spirit seemed to call to him. *Come, climb me and stand upon my summit.* There was magic in this hill. Did Quasia and Cotopa hear the spirit voice? Seemingly not, for they scarcely glanced in its direction.

Once when he was only five winters old his grandfather had helped him climb this hill. Since then he had climbed it many times. From the top he could see the earth spreading in all directions. Somewhere to the east was the Great Water and beyond that white man's land. *What is it like?* Tsena wondered. *And why did they leave it? And why did they come here to our land?*

Beyond Lone Hill they descended gradually into the wide valley of the Llano River and stopped to drink. Then they mounted and rode on—Quasia and Cotopa side by side, talking now and then.

By nightfall they reached the granite shores of the Colorado River. After eating, Tsena wrapped himself in his buffalo robe and lay down beside the fire while the two men smoked Quasia's pipe. Tsena looked up at the stars. In the north he found Hunted Bear, the Three Hunters following him, and finally the Star That Does Not Walk Around.

When the men finished the pipe, Cotopa lay down to sleep, but Quasia sat staring into the coals. Tsena watched him, wondering what kept him up. Soon Cotopa was drawing the deep breaths of sleep.

"You cannot sleep, my son?" Quasia asked in a soft voice.

"Not yet, Father."

"Then I would talk with you." Moving closer, he sat for a moment, his chin propped on his clasped hands.

Is it about Isimanica and the warpath? Tsena wondered.

"I want to tell you about a vision I had three sleeps ago," Quasia began. "I saw an eagle fly up toward the sun. He disappeared and seemed to fly behind it." He turned to look at Tsena. The light of the glowing coals deepened the frown lines. "A breeze stirred the branches of a liveoak tree then, and words of the Great Spirit came to my ears."

"What were they?" Tsena asked without waiting for him to go on.

"The words were, *Make peace.*" Quasia looked back at the coals, nodding to himself.

"The eagle reappeared on the other side of the sun, but—as if he had been singed by the heat—he plummeted to the ground and flew no more."

Tsena felt his own heart plummet. What did it mean? He opened his mouth to ask, but Quasia went on.

"So I must seek peace for the *Nemena.* It is the will of the Great Spirit. And you must be with me—that is why I have brought you along."

"But what does it mean, Father . . . the eagle falling to the ground?"

"I do not know, my son. Still, what danger is there in seeking peace? It is in war that hearts are put to sleep."

4

Tribal Council

On the morning after arriving at Muguara's village, the chiefs of the twelve bands filed into his lodge. Tsena sat down behind his father. Even though he had heard that Muguara was as bald as a river stone, the sight of his shiny greased scalp was a surprise. He had never seen a man with no hair. And this was a huge man who wore many silver rings in his ears. Tsena could not take his eyes off him.

After the pipe was passed, Chief Muguara stood to speak.

"Good and wise chiefs," he began, his voice rumbling like thunder. "Seeing you here fills my heart with joy." He spread his arms as if to embrace them. "I call you together because I have had a sign that the time is right to seek peace with the *tejanos*."

He paused, and there was complete silence. Even the children yelling outside were suddenly quiet.

"They come up the river valleys like the Great Water backing up, spilling over onto our hills. We cannot stop this flow with weapons. We must use words—words of peace."

No wonder he was called the Spirit Talker. His words brought images that Tsena would never forget.

"Let us go and treat with them," he continued. "Let us propose a line that follows the Great Scarp. They shall not cross to build their lodges, and we shall not cross to raid their settlements. What say you, wise men of the council?" He sat down and waited for someone to speak.

It seemed a reasonable idea. Perhaps having the Great Scarp as a line that the *tejanos* could see would keep them away. Tsena looked around the circle. Some of the chiefs were solemnly nodding, while others showed no expression at all. Only Pochana Quoheep, a war chief, frowned.

After a brief silence Quasia stood to speak. "I have long hoped for this moment. Let us do as Muguara says and take the *tejanos* by the hand. According to his vision it is the will of the Great Spirit." He sat down.

Tsena glanced at Pochana Quoheep. His jaws were clenched shut. Clearly he would take no *tejano* by the hand—vision or not. Two other chiefs urged the council to agree with Chief Muguara. And then Pochana Quoheep stood. He was one of the younger chiefs, a wiry, muscular man. His black eyes glittered like jewels in his pocked face.

"Brothers, hear me—for I tell you my heart. The *tejanos* will never stay below the Great Scarp. They long to devour our land, and words will not appease their hunger. I say we must take up the warpath to save our hunting grounds. That is all."

Like Isimanica he did not trust the *tejanos*. Yet unlike Isimanica his hatred did not brim over. He controlled himself like a leader, as Grandfather Ahsenap would say.

After Pochana Quoheep sat down, the chiefs stirred, talking quietly among themselves.

Chief Muguara stood again and waited until every face was turned to him.

"I know how hard it is for youth to listen to the voice of age, but hear me, younger brother. I do not propose that we go to the *tejanos* like newborn calves. No!" he thundered. "I have a plan that gives us the strength of bulls." He passed a hand over his bald head as if smoothing hair that was not there. But it seemed to Tsena that he was soothing himself.

"We hold some of their women and children captive in our villages. The *tejanos* want them back, and they shall have them." A slow smile spread across his face, and he added, "One—by—one. And *only* in return for agreeing to our demands." He paused, looking around the circle.

"I propose we bring in the white girl Matilda," he went on. "The *tejanos* will see for themselves what will happen to other captives if they do not agree. I have spoken."

Quasia stared down at his buffalo robe. A long silence followed. Tsena knew his father did not like Muguara's idea. Would he speak against it? The white girl's face had been scarred by women poking her with burning sticks. Quasia did not approve of such torture and would never allow it in their village.

Finally, Quasia stood and looked directly at Muguara. "To offer only a girl who has been tortured would enrage the *tejanos* and make treating difficult." He turned and addressed all the chiefs. "Hear with your hearts, my brothers. Let us bring in all captives to show our good intentions."

Chief Muguara arose. He fixed Quasia with a steady look.

"You forget, my honored guest, that the girl Matilda was taken captive in revenge for the killing of one of our bravest warriors. It was his mother who touched fire to the girl's face—her right by the law of our fathers. The *tejanos* must see that they cannot kill our warriors and go unpunished."

Around the circle, chiefs nodded agreement.

"He speaks truly," said one.

"Yes," said another, "we must show them our resolve."

Looking at Quasia, Chief Muguara said, "To make peace with the *tejanos* we must run together as one herd." He let his eyes travel around the circle. "Is there agreement for my plan?"

One by one the chiefs nodded. Pochana Quoheep said, "Even though I agree, I will take no part in treating with the *tejanos*."

Only Quasia did not nod. Tsena scarcely breathed as the council waited. Who was right? His father ... or Chief Muguara? Tsena did not like torture either, but if it was done in revenge ... Och, *will I ever be wise enough to know right from wrong?* he wondered.

At last Quasia spoke. "Honored Chief and brothers of the council ... I will run with the herd, but let us keep our eyes open so that we do not plunge over the cliff of hatred." He paused. "I have finished."

Muguara smiled. "So, let three of our number ride to San Antonio de Béxar and tell the *tejanos* we desire to hold council at the next full moon."

That evening a fire was kindled in the center of the village for a feast. Muguara asked Quasia and Tsena to sit on his right in the circle—which was surely an honor. But as Tsena knew, Chief Muguara never did anything without a reason.

Women began passing around trays of roasted meat, boiled potatoes, dried persimmon cakes, and pecans. A young girl came and stood before them, offering a tray of buffalo meat on sticks. She cast a glance at Tsena and looked quickly away.

She was about thirteen, he guessed. A slim girl with luxuriant hair that draped across her shoulders and hung down to her waist. It was as black and shiny as the feathers of a crow.

Chief Muguara turned to them. "This is my beloved granddaughter, Anawakeo." Then to her he said, "And this is Chief Quasia and his son, Tsena."

She smiled and nodded to them.

"Do you not think she is a beauty? Looks like her grandfather." Muguara threw back his head and laughed.

Anawakeo looked down at the tray and smiled. "Grandfather, you embarrass me."

Even Quasia smiled for she was as unlike her grandfather as a doe is to a bear.

"Nonsense, you are pleased—I can tell."

She moved on around the circle then, the fringe on her white doeskin dress swaying as she stepped from person to person and offered the tray with a grace that drew Tsena's eyes. If she looked nothing like her grandfather, she had his same sense of presence. Once she glanced back at Tsena, which made his heart give a little leap.

As they ate, Muguara talked to Quasia.

"You remember my white friend, Wahqua, do you not?"

Quasia nodded, and Tsena turned his attention to the chief, for he was curious about this friend.

43

"He told me many things about white man. He said some are trustworthy and some are not." Muguara chuckled. "Just like our own people." He paused to take a bite of meat and chewed on it for a time.

"So you see," he continued, "since we cannot tell one from the other, we must assume they are all untrustworthy."

Quasia did not reply, which seemed worse than disagreeing. Tsena shifted his legs in the uncomfortable silence. Perhaps this was a good time to ask a question he had been wondering about.

He straightened himself and said, "Chief Muguara, did Wahqua tell you why white men left their land to come here?"

The chief shook his head slowly. "It is a good question, my boy—one I never asked. But whatever their reason, they shall not have our hunting grounds." He said no more, but the question seemed to interest him. Now and then Tsena was aware that the chief was watching him.

Gradually darkness fell upon the village, and the fire cast flickering shadows on nearby lodges.

Chief Muguara stood and said, "Let the dancing begin."

The musicians began to beat their drums. Young people filed into the circle and formed two lines, one for boys and one for girls. Anawakeo glided in and stood with them.

Chief Muguara turned to Tsena. "My granddaughter would be pleased if you would dance with her."

For a moment Tsena's legs seemed paralyzed.

Anawakeo smiled at him, tilting her head to one side. All at once he was on his feet standing opposite her in the boys' line, scarcely aware of how he got there. And then at a loud beat of the drums he was walking toward the girls' line, toward Anawakeo. He stopped before her, his arms hanging at his sides. He had not realized how much taller he was. Her head came only to his shoulders. The little smile lingered on her lips.

"You are tall," she said.

Tsena nodded, but no words came that he could say. He could not say that she was beautiful. *No.* That her way of tilting her head to one side when she smiled made his heart leap. *No, no, no!* Nor could he just stand there stupidly when all around them couples danced to the drumbeat.

"Shall we dance too, or would you rather talk?" she asked, her eyes teasing him.

Tsena grinned. "Dance." He put his hands on her waist, she put hers on his waist, and they stepped to the beat. Soon the music filled him with its rhythm and he forgot himself. When it stopped they changed partners.

Tsena danced with many girls around and around the fire until the musicians set aside their drums. But it was Anawakeo he thought of that night as he lay awake on his bed in Cotopa's lodge. Had she wanted to dance with him, or was it her grandfather's idea?

Prisoners

It was the nineteenth day of the Moon of New Grass—two moons since the tribal council. At last the *Nemena* were on the way to San Antonio de Béxar. The morning sun slanted across the gentle green hills as the procession moved along, keeping the pace of the women pulling travois.

Tsena rode at the front, just behind Quasia, Chief Muguara, and the other chiefs. He looked back at the painted warriors on painted horses. Their silver jewelry glittered in the sunlight. Behind them came the women wearing their beaded dresses. It made his heart swell just to look at the procession. *Surely the* tejanos *will be impressed with our finery*, he thought.

He let his eyes sweep across the women until he found Anawakeo, riding a milk white pony. Her long black hair rippled in the breeze. He was glad Chief Muguara had brought her. Though they had not spoken except for brief greetings, she made the long journey seem short. In fact, he wished it would go on forever.

When Father Sun was halfway up the sky, they mounted a rise. There in the distance Tsena saw San Antonio de Béxar—a cluster of roofs and trees—nestled in a great looping bend of the river. Above all rose a white tower with something gold glinting on its peak.

Quasia turned and motioned Tsena to come ride between him and Chief Muguara. Tsena nudged Yuaneh and eagerly trotted up.

"You have a curious mind, my boy," said the chief, "so I will tell you about this town. People live in square lodges they call *casas*. That tower is called an *iglesia*, and it is where they go to speak to their god—so my white friend told me." He turned to look at the distant town, his bald head shining in the sunlight.

"On top is a golden cross," he went on. "Wahqua said that many winters ago, on the other side of the Great Water, there was a white *puhakut* named Jesus who had strong medicine. But the chief of another tribe took him captive and had him nailed to a cross where he died. Crucify, they call it. So now they put a cross on all *iglesias* to honor his spirit."

"Was he revenged?" Tsena asked.

47

"That I do not know, my boy. You have more questions than I can answer. You need a white friend like mine."

How strange that sounds, thought Tsena.

"Perhaps the best revenge is that his cross is on every *iglesia*," Quasia said.

The two chiefs looked at each other across Tsena. He felt himself pulled between them, between the bow and the string—as if he were the nocked arrow. Then, without a word, they looked straight ahead. There was no more storytelling.

At the river north of Béxar, Muguara raised his arm for a halt and turned to face the procession. "Here we will set up our lodges," he proclaimed in a voice that carried to the very end of it. He sent Cotopa and another warrior into town. "Go and find Colonel Cooke. Tell him we come."

Everyone dismounted, and the travois were unhitched. As the women began setting poles and hoisting lodge covers, Tsena watched Anawakeo help her grandmother. It was too bad they did not live in the same village.

Then he and Quasia led their horses to the river with the other men. His father was quiet as they stood by, but Tsena sensed that he was troubled. Was it because of the captive girl?

During the journey Tsena had seen Matilda for the first time. She usually kept her hand over her nose, but once when she stooped to drink, he had seen it—or what was left of it—and something twisted in his stomach. Her face was a horror, and what made it worse, she must have been a pretty girl—before. Did her father want revenge for revenge? Would it go on and on?

In the time it took to water the horses, a village sprouted up beside the river. They found Topay standing on a crossbar, pinning the top of the lodge cover together.

"There," she said.

Quasia helped her jump down.

"I must bring in our bedding before the voice of thunder says it is time to go." She giggled, covering her mouth with her hand.

Quasia took her by the shoulders. There was a teasing light in his eyes. "The number one wife of a chief does not giggle."

"No, never in public," she said, shaking her head from side to side. "Only in private with my number one husband." She pressed her lips together to keep from laughing.

Then Quasia became serious. "Come inside . . . both of you."

As Tsena ducked through the opening he wondered what his father would say. He had promised to run with the herd. Had he changed his mind?

In the lodge Quasia looked at each of them in turn. "My heart is heavy when I think of the council. I fear the *tejanos* will close their ears to us when they see our captive."

Tsena had guessed right.

Topay put her hands on his shoulders. "You must not worry, my husband. Muguara is a great spirit talker. They will listen."

Quasia looked at her thoughtfully. "I hope so. Still, I am glad we left Chawakeh with your mother."

What does he mean by that? Tsena wondered. *Even if the* tejanos *close their ears, what danger could there be in a peace council?*

Quasia pulled the eagle feather from his scalp lock and put it in her hand. "Here, my wife, I want you to keep this. It will protect you."

She shook her head no and tried to put it back in his scalp lock. But he caught hold of her wrist and said firmly, "You will do as I say."

Topay looked down and bit her lips together. In a moment she tied the feather to the fringe of her dress— over her heart—and let it dangle there.

When the procession formed up, Tsena shouldered his bowcase and mounted Yuaneh. Just downriver was San Antonio de Béxar, with its *casas* and *iglesia* and strange people who had hair on their faces. In spite of his father's concern, excitement stirred in him as they started off. Chief Muguara led the way, with Tsena and Quasia just behind him. Yuaneh pranced and tossed her head as if she felt it too. But underneath that excitement Tsena sensed the slow beat of a drum—or was it his heart?

At the edge of town they entered a street lined with square *casas*. Muguara and Quasia, both proud chiefs, looked neither to the right nor to the left. Tsena tried not to look either, but from the corner of his eye he saw a man step out of a *casa*, and he turned. The man lifted his tall black hat. *Is that a greeting?* he wondered.

On the other side of the street a woman stood in the doorway with a child on her hip. The child waved to Tsena. These people seemed friendly. Did his father notice? Tsena glanced at him, but Quasia kept his eyes straight ahead.

The street opened onto a great plaza where wagons were parked and people had gathered. On the far side loomed the *iglesia*, its tower and cross rising up to the sky. It was larger than Tsena had imagined, making the *casas* and especially the people seem small.

Muguara led them to a *casa* that stood across the plaza from the *iglesia*. There he held up his arm for a halt. Two soldiers stood guard at the doorway, and one of them spoke to someone inside. In a moment a *tejano* chief and a man dressed in buckskin stepped out.

Tsena thought him an elegant chief. Gold fringe hung from the shoulders of his jacket and a long knife swung from his belt. But he did not outshine Chief Muguara in his silver breastplate, ears full of rings, and a red blanket draped around his enormous body. Muguara strode to the *tejano* chief and stood towering over him.

51

The *tejano* chief spoke some words, and the man in buckskin translated, saying, "I am Colonel Cooke."

"I am Muguara, chief of the Twelve Bands. I offer my hand in peace."

They shook hands. Muguara seemed quite at ease in white man's world.

Again Colonel Cooke spoke to the interpreter, who said, "Did you bring in the captives?"

Muguara turned back toward his people. "Bring forth our captive."

A warrior led Matilda toward the chief. She held one hand up to cover her nose. Suddenly, she took her hand away and ran crying to Colonel Cooke.

There was a horrified gasp from the people gathered around. *Father was right*, thought Tsena. The drumbeat inside him quickened.

Colonel Cooke put his arms around her while she sobbed. For a moment the gathering seemed paralyzed. No one spoke or moved. The only sound was Matilda's muffled sobs. Presently the colonel turned the girl over to a soldier, and he led her away, sobbing with her face in her hands.

Only then did anyone stir. Colonel Cooke, his face grim, spoke to the interpreter, and Muguara listened as he translated the words. Then after speaking to Cotopa he announced, "While we chiefs treat with the *tejanos*, our warriors and women will await us in the patio behind the council lodge."

Tsena slumped. Now more than ever he wanted to attend the council with his father. But the chief had spoken. He watched the men file into the doorway. Quasia glanced back and nodded to him. What did he mean? That what he feared was about to happen? Like his vision of the eagle falling to the ground?

Everyone dismounted. Cotopa chose a few boys to watch the horses in the plaza. The others—warriors, women, and children—walked down the street beside the council lodge to the back.

Tsena stroked Yuaneh's neck. "I know there is no grass here, but you must wait for me."

The mare nickered softly.

The patio was surrounded by a line of white posts. Tsena did not want to be enclosed by that pen, but no one else seemed bothered. Not the warriors who lounged around talking and smoking. Not even his mother. Like the other women she spread a hide on the ground and sat down to wait. A few of the younger boys stayed out in the street to play with their small bows and arrows as people of the town gathered around. A *tejano* tossed coins in the air, making a sign for the boys to shoot at them. The boys did, and the *tejanos* shouted when one of them actually hit a coin.

No one else seemed worried.

Anawakeo sat beside her grandmother. Tsena noticed that several warriors were watching her as she arranged her skirt and then shook her long hair like a mane. She seemed to be enjoying their attention. Well, what did he care? All that mattered now was what happened in the council lodge, not here in the patio.

He stalked past her to the back door and peered inside. The chiefs had settled themselves on buffalo robes, Muguara and Quasia in the center. Facing them the *tejanos* sat stiffly in straight chairs. Between the two groups was the interpreter.

There had been no pipe smoked—it was not white man's way, and this was his council lodge. But from the looks of Colonel Cooke's face, they should have smoked first so that there would be good will between them.

Colonel Cooke was talking. When he finished, he nodded to the interpreter and listened as his words were translated.

"I am Colonel Cooke. On my left is Colonel McLeod, and on my right is Colonel Fisher. We and the leaders of this town are glad you seek peace. We hope an agreement can be reached to stop the fighting between us."

His words did not match his expression.

Chief Muguara, placing his hands on his knees and holding his head high, spoke next. "My face shines with joy as I look upon you and hear your words of welcome. Our hearts beat for peace even as yours. Father Sun hears me, Mother Earth hears me. They know that I tell the truth."

There was a long pause, as if the *tejanos* did not believe Muguara's words.

At last Colonel Cooke spoke.

"Where are the other captives you promised to bring?" the interpreter said.

Muguara drew himself up and spaced his words carefully.

"We have brought in the only one we had."

It was a lie. *He speaks with a forked tongue*, thought Tsena.

Muguara paused, turning first right, then left to run his eyes over the chiefs on either side. "It is true that there are more captives, but they are held by other bands." He waited for the interpreter to translate his words.

"For the captive we have brought in," Muguara went on, "we want four woolen blankets, four of the new guns that have a shot for each finger of the hand, and vermilion paint."

The colonel made no response, so he continued.

"For the remainder of the captives there is a higher price." His words resonated within the stone walls. Looking steadily at Colonel Cooke, he added, "How do you like the answer?"

The colonel did not say, but Tsena could see by the way his eyes flashed that he did not like it at all. And neither did Colonel Fisher. He stood abruptly, strode to the front door, and spoke to the guard standing outside. A company of soldiers marched into the council lodge with guns clutched across their chests and took positions around the walls, blocking the two doors. At the same time another company stationed themselves along the white posts in back.

The drumbeat inside Tsena pounded furiously. What was happening?

Standing on tiptoes, he peered around the soldier in the doorway. The chiefs stirred about and spoke among themselves. A few took hold of their bows, others their knives. Tsena reached back and pulled out his bow and an arrow.

Colonel Cooke spoke to the interpreter, whose body stiffened. His eyes were wide like a prairie dog about to dive into his tunnel.

"No!" he replied, shaking his head. "No!"

The colonel's face turned red. He jumped up, pointed at Chief Muguara, and spoke angrily.

The interpreter's mouth opened, but no words came out. He began to edge toward the front door as he looked from the colonel to Muguara. When he reached it, he suddenly blurted out the words.

"Colonel Cooke says there will be no ransom paid for captives."

Here the interpreter faltered, glanced back at the colonel, who nodded for him to proceed, and took a deep breath. "He says your women and children may depart in peace. Your warriors may go back to your camps and return with the captives. Until then . . ." He looked out the open door to the plaza. "Until then, all the chiefs are our prisoners." He turned and fled.

The Promise

Prisoners! The word pierced Tsena like an arrow. Father—a prisoner?

The chiefs leaped up, stringing bows, nocking arrows, yelling, "*Aieeeee! Aieeeee!*" Quasia signaled Tsena to go. Chief Pakawa ran for the back door, his knife in hand. The soldier moved to block his way. Pakawa lunged at him and drove it into his chest. The soldier staggered back, clutching the knife, and fell at Tsena's feet.

Blam came a shot from inside, and Pakawa sprawled on top of the soldier. Tsena stared at the blood gushing from the chief's back, and for one breathless moment he could not move.

Then a *tejano* shouted. Gunfire echoed in the council

57

lodge. *Blam, blam, blam!* Tsena peered inside, looking for Quasia, but soldiers blocked his view. The room was filled with smoke. Had his father escaped out the front door?

Tsena turned back toward the patio. Anawakeo was struggling to help her grandmother up. He ran to them and pulled the old woman to her feet. For an instant Anawakeo thanked him with her eyes. Then people crowded against them, between them, and he lost sight of her. Women screamed and pushed to escape. Soldiers fired into the crowd. Where was his mother? Tsena struggled to nock an arrow.

As the scrambling mass of people reached the white pen it gave way, and they surged into the street. With room to move Tsena raised his bow and shot at one of the soldiers, but the arrow flew over his head.

In the plaza he looked around for his father and mother and Anawakeo in the confusion of people running in every direction. Where were they? Yuaneh and all the horses were gone—probably scattered at the first shots.

Then from behind someone caught hold of his arm. He spun around. "Mother!"

Her eyes were wild with terror. "Your father, where is he?"

Tsena glanced about frantically, searching for that familiar tall figure. And then he saw Quasia burst out of the council lodge.

"There he is!" Tsena said.

"Quasia!" shouted Topay, and together they dashed toward him, pushing through the crowd.

He saw them coming and grabbed Topay by the arm. "The river ... run for the river!" he shouted to Tsena.

They ran down a narrow street, Tsena following with an arrow nocked on his bow. A few women hurried along, pulling or carrying their children, but no Anawakeo or her grandmother.

Suddenly, from out of a side street, a mounted *tejano* rode into their path. His horse reared, and the *tejano* pointed a pistol and fired. Quasia pitched backward, holding his chest.

With Topay's scream in his ears, Tsena pulled the bowstring and shot. The arrow drove into the man's shoulder. The *tejano* charged his horse, kicked the bow from Tsena's hand, and thrust the gun at him. For one splinter of time Tsena stared into its terrible little eye. Everything seemed to stop still—the horse, the man, the people in the street.

He reached out, grabbed hold of the barrel, and pulled. It came off in his hand. He staggered back, trying to keep his balance, but he fell. At that moment fire exploded in the *tejano's* face, splattering him with blood. He tumbled off the horse and did not move.

Tsena scrambled up, still clutching the gun barrel, and ran to his father. Topay hovered over him, covering his wound with one bloody hand, caressing his face with the other. Quasia stared at her, mouth open.

Is Father dying? Tsena dropped to his knees. "We have to get him away!" he said, looking over his shoulder.

In the street, warriors backed toward the river with their bows ready. The *tejano's* horse whinnied and reared, but his reins were caught, wrapped around the dead man's arm. The horse tried to back away. His eyes were big, showing their whites. He dragged the body a short distance and reared again.

Tsena got to his feet. He needed that horse. Sticking the barrel in his belt, he edged close to the frightened animal and took the reins. "Hoh," he said in a low voice as he unwrapped them.

"Run!" screamed a woman who was hurrying by with her two children in hand. "The *tejanos* come."

The horse shied, but Tsena held him, stroking his neck, speaking to him.

Once across the street, he tied the reins to a post. He knelt and got his arm under his father's shoulder while Topay lifted him on the other side. To Tsena's relief Quasia stirred and raised himself up on one elbow with a grunt. He pressed his hand to his chest.

"I can walk," he muttered, struggling to his feet. His legs buckled, and the trickle of blood became a stream.

As more people ran by, a warrior stopped. It was Cotopa. He shouldered his bow and helped lift Quasia into the saddle. Topay got on behind and held him around the chest. His head slumped forward.

"Hurry," Cotopa urged, "there is bad medicine. Chief Muguara has been slain." Then he nocked an arrow and turned to face the rear.

Tsena grabbed up his bow and led the horse toward the river at a trot. His mind was filled with a jumble of thoughts. *Muguara is dead. Will Father die too? Where is Anawakeo? If only Yuaneh were here instead of this big lumbering beast . . .*

When they came to the river, Quasia lifted his head. "Stop."

"But Father, the *tejanos* come."

He looked hard at Tsena, summoning his strength. "Stop!"

There was no disobeying his command.

Tsena found a place on the river where heavy underbrush would hide them. He tied the horse, took a blanket roll from behind the saddle, and spread it on the ground. Together they helped Quasia down onto the blanket. More gunshots sounded from the town.

Topay wadded her skirt and pressed it to his chest. Still the blood flowed. His face had become strangely pale.

"I would . . . speak with you," Quasia said, his voice barely more than a whisper. "My spirit flies away."

"*No-o-o-o-o*, Quasia, don't leave me." Topay began to weep, laying her head over the bloody wound.

Tsena sank to his knees. His throat ached as he watched life drain out of his father.

"They will kill us all," Quasia said, putting his hand on Topay's head. "You ... the love of my life ... and you, my beloved son ..."

Topay lifted her head and looked into his eyes, clutching his shoulders as if she would not let him go.

"Surrender," he whispered. Then, turning to Tsena, he said, "Make peace with them."

"Father, I cannot." His voice sounded choked.

"You must." Quasia's eyes lighted with a sudden intensity. He looked at his wife on one side, then at his son on the other, seeming to hold them with his eyes. "Promise ..."

When they did not reply immediately, he raised himself up on his elbow. "Promise," he demanded. Blood appeared at the corner of his mouth and trickled down his chin.

Topay nodded silently.

"I promise, Father," said Tsena.

Quasia fell back, his mouth open, eyes closed. A shudder passed through him.

"*No-o-o-o-o, no-o-o-o-o!*" Topay screamed as she fell over him and clung to his body.

Tsena felt as if he were Lone Hill. All around him the world had gone black. How long he sat there listening to his mother's sobs he did not know. He scarcely knew where he was or what had happened. He found himself staring at his father's gaping mouth.

He could not be dead. Any moment he would draw a breath and get up. Tsena put his hand on Quasia's shoulder.

"He is still warm, Mother!" he whispered.

Topay sat back and looked at Tsena, her face contorted, her dark eyes melting in tears. She shook her head from side to side. His eyes began to melt too. His father might still be warm, but the breath of life had gone out of him.

From behind came the snap of a twig. Tsena jerked around. A young soldier approached, his long gun ready.

"Take off your bow," he ordered in Spanish.

Tsena fingered the strap of his bowcase, his thoughts leaping ahead. *Reach in the quiver . . . pull out an arrow . . . plunge it into his heart.*

But he remembered his promise.

Slowly, he lifted the strap, lay the bowcase on the ground, and stood. With his chin up, he looked at the soldier. For a moment no words came. Then he heard himself speaking Spanish. "My mother and I not fight."

It was as if someone else had spoken.

7

All Dead

The soldier motioned with his gun. "Get up, squaw."

Topay shook her head. "I cannot leave him here," she told Tsena. She leaned over Quasia and caressed his face.

Tsena halfway expected his father's arms to reach up and embrace her.

"I say *get up!*" the soldier yelled, coming closer.

Tsena stiffened. "*Un momento,*" he said.

The soldier's mouth opened, but he did not speak. His eyes shifted to Topay.

Tsena knelt beside her. She sat up and looked at him as if to ask, *Is this truly happening?* He nodded yes. Then gently lifting his father's body, Tsena pulled the blanket from underneath him. Topay sat with her hand covering her mouth as Tsena prepared to cover him.

Suddenly, she pulled off her necklace of silver beads and blue stones—the one Quasia had given her—and put it around his neck. "Farewell, my Quasia, my heart," she whispered.

"Come, Mother," Tsena said, slowly spreading the blanket over his father.

"*Ahora, vamonos,*" barked the soldier. He motioned with his gun for them to move.

Helping Topay stand, Tsena led her around the undergrowth and up the embankment. At the top she slumped. He stopped and put her arm over his shoulder.

"*Adelante,*" the soldier commanded from behind and prodded her with the barrel.

Tsena swung around and glared. *"No tocar otra vez!"*

The soldier looked at him a moment, his lips pressed together. Then with an upward jerk of his head he said, "*Adelante.*"

Tsena started walking toward the plaza with Topay stumbling along at his side. If he had not held her up she would have fallen. The *Nemena* lay wounded or dead in the street. *Tejanos* ran about, stopping to turn over a body or fire another bullet. There was Cotopa. And there Tasiwaw with her little son sprawled beside her. *This is not possible*, thought Tsena. *Surely Cotopa will get up and run down the street. In a moment Tasiwaw's child will begin to cry. And from the river Father will call us to come back.*

When they reached the plaza, several soldiers crowded around, pushing the two of them past the council lodge to the next doorway and down a dark passage. The sound of women wailing came from somewhere inside the walls. Tsena lurched from side to side as soldiers shoved, shouting words he could not understand.

At the end of the passage, a soldier opened another door. There behind bars were *Nemena* women and children. Some tore at their hair and clothes as they wailed. Children huddled beside their mothers while the older ones sat dazed and staring. Tsena looked about quickly, searching for Anawakeo—and found her. She sat beside her grandmother at the back of the room. At least they were alive.

The soldiers made way for a small *mexicano*. With a jangling of keys he unlocked the barred door. Hands shoved Tsena and his mother inside. The door clanked shut.

Tsena remained standing, but Topay sank to the dirt floor. None of the twelve chiefs, none of the warriors were here. *Have some escaped?* Tsena wondered. *Will they come back and free us? Will anything ever be the same?*

At last he sat down and listened to the women. Their wailing swirled around him. He closed his eyes and let himself be carried on their voices, out of the dark room, back to the village . . .

Suddenly, there was a jangle of keys and the barred door creaked open. The *mexicano* pushed Napawat, an old blind warrior, inside. He stood listening for a moment until everyone was quiet.

Then he said, "All dead—the great chiefs, the warriors—all dead."

The women renewed their wailing. "All dead ... all dead."

After a while Anawakeo came to Tsena and knelt. "Grandmother wishes me to speak to you." She looked at her hands clasped tightly in her lap. Then, looking up, she said, "Tsena, I am afraid they will kill us too." She put her face down in her hands.

Her dark hair fell across her cheeks like a mane. Tsena wanted to reach out and stroke it as he would Yuaneh to comfort her. Somehow her fear made him feel less afraid. He must not let anything happen to her.

In a moment Anawakeo smoothed back her hair and looked up. "Grandmother will not forget your kindness ... and neither will I." A sad smile flicked at the corners of her mouth and disappeared. "She wants you to be our leader. She wants you to persuade the *tejanos* to let us go."

He felt himself smile back at her and nod. Yes, he would talk to the *tejanos*. That is what Father wanted— what he, Tsena, had promised. He would talk, yes. He would do whatever it took to get Anawakeo, her grandmother, his mother—all of them—out of here. But never, never would he make peace.

"You smile and then you frown," Anawakeo said.

"Do not worry," he said. "Tell your grandmother that I will speak to them. Tell her I will ask the Great Spirit to put words in my mouth."

A light came to her eyes. "I will, Tsena."

For a moment they looked at each other without speaking. Then she stood and returned to her grandmother.

All afternoon women continued their wailing. A few lay on the dirt floor, exhausted. Topay sat with her head cradled in her hands, moaning softly.

From the other side of the door Tsena could hear *tejanos* talking, sometimes shouting. Though only Anawakeo had said it aloud, he knew all the women feared they would be killed. And in his boy's heart, he did too. But he could not be a boy any longer.

He looked over at Napawat, who sat alone, rocking back and forth. *Maybe he has some wise words to help me*, he thought, and made his way to the old man.

Napawat stopped rocking and turned his face in Tsena's direction. "Who is there?" he asked.

"It is Tsena, son of . . . of Chief Quasia. May I speak?"

There was a slight nod.

"The women have asked me to try to persuade the *tejanos* to free us. I think they should have asked you, who are older and wiser."

Napawat stirred. He reached out, ran his fingers over Tsena's face, and let his hand come to rest on his shoulder. For a long time he said nothing. Tsena looked at his clouded eyes, at his nose laced with spidery veins, at his matted gray hair. How sad to be both old and blind—except that maybe he did not fear dying.

At last Napawat spoke. "I am an old man, my boy. The women know you have something that I have lost. You have strength. Show the *tejanos* strength—not anger." He began rocking again. "Not anger," he repeated. "That is all."

Tsena thanked him and went back to his place near the bars. *Show them strength, not anger. But how?* Tsena wondered. *Begging will not work—or demanding. What then? How am I to follow Napawat's advice? What are the words I must speak?*

Taking his medicine bag in hand, he whispered, "Hear me, Great Spirit, put words in my mouth that will open the ears of the *tejanos*."

He sat listening to his mind for a long time. And then two words came to him: *white captives*. Yes, of course. Use the white captives to make a bargain.

So far, he realized, the *Nemena* knew nothing of what had happened here. When they found out . . . what would they do? Take revenge on the white captives. Kill them. *Unless . . . unless we are returned unharmed*, he thought. Perhaps the captives would be killed anyway. Still, he was going to promise what he could not truthfully promise: release us and the white captives will be spared.

Tsena began to plan what he would say the next day. His words must be eloquent to impress the *tejanos*. As darkness crept over the room, he said them over and over.

It was late when he lay back on the dirt floor. He put his hand on the gun barrel inside his belt. It did not matter that it poked his stomach. It was a coup trophy, and he would keep it always.

Through the barred window a few stars were visible. He longed to see the Star That Does Not Walk Around, for it was the only thing in his life that had not changed. Even Anawakeo was different. He remembered the way her eyes shone at him. He could not see her in the darkness, but he could feel her presence.

From Where the Sun Now Stands

Tsena awoke. Someone was banging on the bars, yelling, "*Desayuno*, breakfast." The noise drove all thoughts from his head. He sat up and clamped his hands over his ears. It was the *mexicano*.

At last he stopped banging, and in the sudden quiet, thoughts came flooding back. Father was gone . . . all the chiefs were gone. And he was a prisoner in this dark, foul-smelling room where they had to relieve themselves in a pot behind a hanging blanket.

Yet Father Sun had risen again and cast a square of light high on the opposite wall. And there was food to eat.

The *mexicano* slipped trays under the barred door. As women passed them around, children squealed, reaching out for slices of bread and bowls of beans.

Tsena stood and walked between them to the bars. Looking down at the small *mexicano*, he said, *"Quiero hablar con Colonel Cooke."* (I want to speak with Colonel Cooke.)

The man's mustache twitched. "How many years do you have?"

"Ten and six."

The *mexicano* snorted. "He does not speak with children." He turned and shut the outer door.

Tsena stood for a moment, his body rigid, thinking of Napawat's words: *Show them strength, not anger.*

One of the women brought a tray, and he sat down. He had to make himself eat, for he had no hunger. Still, he needed strength.

When the small square of sunlight had crept down the wall onto the floor, the outer door opened, and in stepped the three colonels. With them was the prairie dog interpreter.

Colonel Cooke, standing tall and erect, said, "Who speaks for your people?"

Tsena drew himself up. "I do."

The colonel said something to the other two, and they laughed.

Tsena watched them without expression. How he hated their laughter.

The colonel spoke through the interpreter again. "You are still a child," he said.

Tsena did not answer until their faces were sober. Then in a steady voice he said, "Now that all our chiefs and warriors are gone, I speak for them."

The women began to wail again.

"My father was a great chief who sought only peace," he went on.

The colonels listened as his words were translated. For a moment they remained silent. The women's wailing filled the room.

Colonel Cooke spoke angry words. "Tell them to . . ." the interpreter hesitated, "to stop."

"They cannot stop grieving," Tsena replied.

The colonel flashed a look at him and called for the *mexicano*. He unlocked the door, grabbed Tsena by the arm, and led him along the passage to another room where there were no bars. It had windows that opened onto the deserted plaza.

"Sit," he said, pushing him toward a chair.

But Tsena sat instead on the floor and folded his legs. He would not sit in white man's way.

The three colonels entered and settled themselves in chairs facing him with the interpreter between.

Colonel Cooke said, "Are you ready to bring in the remaining captives?"

Tsena's heart began to pound. He took a deep breath and spoke the words he had memorized. "Our people wait in the hills for us to return. When the wind carries the cries of our women to them, a terrible storm will break over the heads of the captives."

Colonel Cooke's face reddened as he listened to the interpreter.

"Threatening us, are you, boy?"

"No," he replied, though that was exactly what he was doing and he knew it—relished it. "I am offering a solution." He paused to let the words be translated. "Only the chiefs' wives have the power to spare the captives. Therefore I say, let us return to our camp and scatter the storm clouds."

To Tsena's surprise, Colonel Cooke tilted his head back and began to laugh. The other colonels laughed with him, making the gold fringe on their shoulders quiver. Tsena watched and listened, his face rigid. It did not sound like real laughter. It was forced.

Suddenly, the colonel became serious. "Fancy yourself an orator, eh? You must have taken lessons from old Muguara. But he—as we say—spoke out of two sides of his mouth. Why should we believe you now?"

It is true, thought Tsena. *Muguara tried to fool the* tejanos. *Still, that is no excuse for taking prisoners during a council. Och, they are all to blame—all except Father.* He remembered how Quasia tried to persuade the tribal council to bring in all the captives. If only they had listened.

All at once the words in his heart came pouring out.

"My father, Chief Quasia, never took a white captive . . . never. He urged the tribal council to return them all, but . . ." His voice broke, and he turned away. The *tejanos* must not see such weakness.

Except for the distant sound of wailing, there was silence in the room. Blinking hard, he tried to clear his eyes without wiping them.

Finally, the colonel spoke in a quiet voice. "I believe you are telling the truth," the interpreter translated. "What is your name?"

"Tsena," he answered, facing the colonel again.

"It would have been wiser, Tsena, if they had listened to your father. Perhaps now they will follow his advice."

Hope leaped up in Tsena's heart. "Yes, they will listen to my mother and the other chiefs' wives. Release us so we can speak to them before it is too late."

He watched as they talked among themselves. Colonel Fisher sounded angry. At last Colonel Cooke leaned back, stuck his thumbs under his belt, and spoke.

"We have decided to let one of the women go and tell your people that when all the captives are brought in, we will release you."

"Only one?" Tsena asked.

"Yes, one—your mother," said the colonel. "Now, go and tell her that we will provide a horse and food for the journey."

The *mexicano*, two soldiers, and the interpreter

escorted him back to the prison room and stood waiting outside the bars.

Will Mother agree to go alone? Tsena wondered. *Probably not. But she must! How can I convince her?*

He took a deep breath and said, "They will release only one of us. It is you they choose, Mother."

She shook her head and looked down.

Kneeling beside her, he said, "Please . . . they want you to take word that the rest of us will be freed as soon as the captives are returned—unharmed."

Topay sat, rubbing her hands up and down on her bloodied skirt. "I cannot leave you here, my son. They will not listen to me anyway."

"It is our only hope, Mother. And it is what Father wanted. Do it for him and for Chawakeh."

She lifted her face and looked straight at Tsena. After a moment she said quietly, "All right, I will go."

He turned to the interpreter. "She will go."

Later, when Father Sun had reached the zenith, the *mexicano* and the soldiers returned. They allowed Tsena to accompany Topay out to the corral behind the council lodge. A group was gathered there—the colonels, the interpreter, and a soldier holding the reins of a small gray horse.

"How long will it take you to go and return?" the interpreter asked.

Topay looked at Tsena.

"Perhaps five sleeps," he said.

Then Colonel Cooke spoke and watched Topay as his words were translated.

"Tell your people that from where the sun now stands, you have twelve sleeps to bring in the captives. If you do not return in that time, we will put the prisoners to death."

His mother's face looked stricken. She untied the eagle feather from the fringe of her dress. "Here, my son, this will protect you."

◇nly ◇oyote 𝒦nows

Two sleeps later Tsena stood with the other prisoners outside the walls of Mission San José, waiting for the heavy wooden gates to open. The Old Ones and the young children sat in an oxcart. Their escort, two companies of mounted soldiers, waited also while the horses swished their tails and snorted impatiently.

Earlier that day soldiers had taken them out of the prison room and through the streets of Béxar, where people stood to watch them pass by. The procession had moved south across the rolling countryside to the crest of this gentle hill.

Now the sun was halfway down the sky. A bank of clouds hovered across the horizon in the north, moving this way on a cold wind that swept across the hill. The Old Ones pulled their robes and blankets closer around them.

It was good to be out of the prison room, Tsena thought, to feel the warmth of the sun on his face and the sharp cut of the wind. But unlike the wind, he was not free. They were waiting to enter a new prison. He looked over at Anawakeo, who stood on the other side of the oxcart. She must have sensed his attention, for she turned to look at him, tilting her head to one side as if asking him to dance.

He smiled and nodded.

She looked away then, but Tsena let his eyes rest on her. He remembered dancing with her, his hands on her waist, and for a moment he forgot the threat that hung over them all.

Suddenly, old Napawat said, "Tell me what your eyes see, my boy."

Startled, Tsena glanced up at the blind man sitting in the oxcart. *Surely he could not tell I was looking at Anawakeo. Or could he?* One thing was sure. The fresh air had brought the old man back to life.

"Tell me what sort of place they are putting us in," he went on. "Be my eyes."

"Yes, Old One, I will try."

Tsena looked about. "We stand in front of a gate in a stone wall that is as tall as three men. And beyond the wall I can see the tower of an *iglesia* rising even higher— pointing to the sky."

Napawat nodded. "Your words paint pictures, my young friend."

Just then the gates swung open, and the officer in the lead called, "*Vamonos!*"

Tsena walked beside the cart, whispering to Napawat. "Now we pass through the gate, Old One. Soldiers are watching us from the top of the wall."

Inside the gate they halted. Tsena looked up at the *iglesia*. "We are in a great square space. The *iglesia* rises up in front of us. Around its doorway are stone people— almost life-size." He looked around the square. "It is like a white man's village. The walls are lined with flat-topped lodges. There are trees and grass—even a creek. And soldiers stand about everywhere."

An officer in a blue uniform, his long knife wagging at his side, strode toward them and stopped. It was Colonel Fisher. He was not a tall man, but he held him-self erect, and from under the bill of his soldier cap his eyes fastened on Tsena.

Tsena stiffened. This was the man who had called the soldiers into the council lodge. If not for him, Father would be alive—*all* the chiefs would be alive.

"Nine days remain for your people to return the captives," the colonel said in Spanish.

Yes, thought Tsena, *and how many will it take for you to return my father?*

"Until then," Colonel Fisher continued, "we keep you here in the mission. There are no locks on your doors. In the day you can go out, but at night you stay inside." He waved an arm toward the wall. "Guards walk along the walls at all times. They shoot anybody who tries to escape. *Comprende?*"

Tsena felt anger rising inside. He tilted his head back and clenched his jaws.

Colonel Fisher put a hand on his long knife and said, "Do not lift your nose at me, savage, unless you want it cut off!"

Slowly Tsena lowered his chin—but not his eyes.

"Better," said the colonel. "Now go with Captain Redd."

The Old Ones and the children climbed out of the cart. Tsena gripped Napawat's bony arm to support him as they followed Captain Redd.

"Take care, my boy, do not show them your anger," Napawat said in a low voice. "The time for revenge will come." He moved his arm about. "Besides, my arm goes numb."

"Forgive me, Old One. But it is better that I choke your arm than his throat."

Napawat chuckled. "Now you speak wisely, Young One."

The captain led them along the row of wall lodges. He walked with long, loose strides—like Father, Tsena thought—and the likeness struck deep inside him.

When they reached a door near the corner of the square, Captain Redd opened it and turned to Tsena, his eyes kind—again like Father.

"You are the boy called Tsena?" he asked.

Tsena nodded.

"Lo siento por su padre."

Tsena stared at him, wondering if he had understood the Spanish words. *Lo siento*—he knew that meant *I am sorry.* And *padre* was *father*, of course. I am sorry about your father. For a moment he did not move or speak. *To think that a* tejano *is sorry for Father's death . . .*

Tsena looked down and said, *"Gracias."*

The captain motioned toward the door. "You here with the old man."

Tsena nodded and watched him move on to the next door and the next, assigning women to their quarters. This man was surely different from other *tejanos.*

Then Captain Redd pointed to a tall stone lodge beside the main gate. "When the bell rings, come there. You get food after the soldiers eat." He nodded once and strode away.

"Well, Old One," said Tsena when they were inside their room, "if we must be prisoners, this is better than where we were. We have a friendly captain and a room with a fire pit in the corner and two beds."

"Good," Napawat said, "I shall lie down now and rest."

After Tsena helped him to a bed, he took the gun barrel from his belt and hid it in a crack over the window. It would be safe there until they left this place. Then he stepped outside.

The children had already found something to play on—a stone oven in front of their quarters. On the far side of the square a group of soldiers sat on benches, polishing their guns. Near the center an old cottonwood tree grew by the creek. Since no soldiers were there, Tsena walked over to the creek, knelt and scooped up some water. It was clear and sweet. He took another drink and washed his face. Then he sat down beside the tree, glad for a few moments to himself.

From the direction of the *iglesia* he heard a horse whinny, and it set him to wondering about Yuaneh. Had she been captured by some *tejano*? And if so, how was he treating her? Tsena leaned back against the rough trunk. He thought about his mother. Could she persuade the chiefs to bring in the captives? He wanted to believe she could. But he feared that the desire for revenge would be too strong.

All at once he thought of Napawat. Coyote was his guardian spirit, and a person with coyote medicine could see into the future. *I will ask him tonight*, Tsena decided.

Hearing soft steps, he sat up quickly. It was Anawakeo. She knelt beside the creek, filling a jug. Back in the village, if a boy wanted to see a girl alone he would wait at the place where she filled her water bag. If she gave him a glance, it meant she liked him.

As Anawakeo started back Tsena felt his heart leap, for she paused and gave him that sidelong glance.

"Wait," he said and stood.

She stepped nearer so that the tree hid them from the others, and looked up at him.

"It is good here—in the mission, I mean," she said.

"Yes, almost like a village."

She smiled and looked away. "I have to go . . ."

"Wait, not yet," he said. It had been easier to talk when she came to him in the prison room, crying.

She waited, tilting her head to one side and looking at him.

"Are you still afraid?" he asked.

"Yes, but now I have hope."

Tsena nodded. "I . . . I won't let anything happen to you, Anawakeo." He felt the blood rush to his face. It was the first time he had called her by name.

She smiled. "You make my heart glad, Tsena." Then she turned and almost ran back to her room.

The dark bank of clouds slowly spread across the sky, and the north wind swooped over the walls and down into the square. After the bell rang, Tsena, Napawat, and the women and children walked to the big stone lodge. They sat on the ground outside, huddled in blankets, and waited for the soldiers to finish supper.

Finally, when the last soldiers left the building and scattered across the square to their quarters, a *mexicano* stepped out the door and motioned for them to come inside. He pointed to a table near the door of the vast room. There they picked up bowls of something called *masa de maíz* and went outside to eat.

"It should be called yellow vomit," Tsena whispered to Napawat. "If this is what they feed their warriors, then we have nothing to fear."

The old man chuckled. "Call it what you will, Young One, but eat it."

After supper Tsena gathered some dry grass and a dead branch from under the cottonwood tree and hurried back to the room. Napawat took out his fire drill and twirled the stick until sparks jumped onto the grass. Tsena blew gently, making them glow at first and then burst into a flame.

Outside, rain began to fall. The two sat silently as Tsena added twigs. He looked at the old warrior. His nose was a ridge between his sunken eyes.

"I have heard from the women that you have coyote medicine," Tsena said.

Napawat turned his face toward him. "You want to know the future, do you?"

"Yes, Old One."

Napawat held his hands to the fire and rubbed them together. "Coyote will not call to me here inside these walls."

"But you have the wisdom of many winters. What can you tell me? Will our people return the captives?"

"First I will have my pipe. It is the only pleasure left to an old blind man." He reached under his shirt and pulled out a pouch. "Fill it for me, boy."

"Yes, Old One."

When Napawat had drawn a few puffs, he said, "Our great chiefs have all been killed—all those who wanted peace with white man. Now only the hot bloods remain, and they will want revenge. That much I know. But whether they will return the captives I cannot say. Only Coyote knows."

"And what if they don't, Old One, what then? Will the *tejanos* kill us like Colonel Cooke said?"

Napawat puffed quietly on his pipe.

"I know little of the hearts of white men, my boy, but it is said that their *puhakut*, the one called Jesus, told them to love their enemy."

"Love their enemy?" Tsena almost shouted. "Surely you heard wrong, Old One. How could any man love his enemy?"

Napawat shrugged.

"*Tejanos* don't love their enemies," Tsena went on. "They *kill* them." He got up and paced about the room.

"Then perhaps, my young hot-blooded one, we should make friends with them while we are their prisoners." He tapped his pipe against the hearth, emptying the bowl. "I am old. I have lived a long life and have little to lose. But you have much to lose, Young One."

Then slowly, painfully, he hoisted himself up. "Now I grow weary."

Tsena came and helped him to the bed, but for himself there could be no sleep. How could he make friends with Colonel Fisher? Outside he heard the step of the guards passing by, and then all was quiet except for the rain that pattered on the flat roof and dripped from the water spout.

Love your en-e-my, the dripping seemed to say. *Love your en-e-my.*

He covered his ears with his hands.

An Old Friend

In the next days Tsena thought about Napawat's words. But whenever he saw Colonel Fisher—even from across the square—he felt anger begin to stir inside. The only *tejano* he could imagine befriending was Captain Redd.

One morning after the soldiers had finished their marching about the square, he heard shouts coming from the main gate. Someone lay on the ground while others crowded around. Staying close to the wall lodges, Tsena hurried to see what had happened and stopped a short distance away. It seemed that the man had fallen from the wooden platform above the gate. As Tsena watched, two soldiers brought a litter, lifted the man onto it, and carried him to his quarters. It was Colonel Fisher.

Good! thought Tsena. *Let him rot in his bed.*

Soon a soldier bolted out of the colonel's door and leaped on his horse. As the gates swung open, he galloped off toward Béxar. All around the square, soldiers gathered in little groups to talk. The children went back to their play in the far corner.

Tsena sat down near the main gate, watching and pondering. Did this change anything? Would the colonel leave the mission?

When the sun had risen halfway up the sky, the gates were opened again. In rode the soldier on Colonel Fisher's horse with another rider—a stout man with bushy brown hair growing on his upper lip. *Mustache*, white men called it. Tsena wondered how a man could eat and drink with such a bush on his lip.

The two dismounted in front of the colonel's quarters and went inside. For a long time nothing more happened. Tsena grew tired of waiting and started back to his quarters. Then he stopped and listened. The sound of trotting horses came from outside the wall. A lot of them, coming closer. Two soldiers lifted the bar and opened the gates.

Suddenly, a high-pitched whinny pierced the air, ending in a low rumble. Tsena caught his breath. He knew that whinny as well as he knew his grandfather's voice.

Captain Redd and a group of soldiers rode through the gate, leading horses, but Tsena saw only the one

89

following the captain—a red mare with golden mane and tail.

"Yuaneh!" he shouted.

The mare lifted her head, ears pricked. Tsena took a few steps, and Yuaneh reared up, whinnying again. Without a thought he ran toward her. He heard a shout, and something struck him on the side of the head. He staggered, plunging headlong into darkness.

How long he stayed there he did not know, but slowly, slowly he became aware of a voice from far away saying, "Tsena? Wake up, Tsena."

He groped his way up through the heavy darkness and struggled to open his eyes. Blinking and squinting into the brightness, he saw Anawakeo leaning over him. Captain Redd and the stout man knelt on his other side. For a moment he could not understand. Why did his head ache? Why was he lying on the ground? Why were all these people and horses standing around him?

"Tsena," Anawakeo whispered. "Thank the spirits."

"What . . . what happened?" His tongue felt thick.

"They hit you with a gun." She lay a cool, damp cloth across his forehead. "They think you were trying to escape."

"Escape?" He turned to look at Captain Redd.

"Lucky you did not get killed," said the captain in Spanish.

Then Tsena heard a horse snorting, shaking its reins, and he remembered. He had been running toward Yuaneh.

He sat up and his head throbbed. There she was. "Yuaneh!" he cried.

Yuaneh tossed her head and backed away as two men struggled to hold her. Tsena started up, but the captain put a hand on his shoulder.

"Whoa, *muchacho*," he said.

Tsena sat back.

"You know that horse?" the captain asked.

"*Sí*, my horse, Yuaneh. I run to her—not to the gate."

A slow grin spread across Captain Redd's face. "Then maybe you can make her quiet." He turned to the man beside him. "Is *bueno*, Doctor?"

The doctor looked closely at Tsena from under his bushy eyebrows. There was kindness in his face.

"You have pain here?" He pointed to the side of his head.

"No," Tsena lied.

The doctor chuckled. "Well, try to stand up then."

With the doctor holding one arm and Captain Redd the other, he stood. For a moment his knees felt like yellow vomit, but he straightened his back and took a deep breath.

Anawakeo stood too. "What do they say?" she asked.

"They want me to calm Yuaneh."

"They are not going to . . . punish you?"

"No."

She smiled. "I will tell the others." She flung her long hair around and ran back to the women.

Tsena released himself from Captain Redd and the doctor and started toward Yuaneh saying, "Hoh ..." She lowered her head and waited for him.

Forgetting the soldiers, forgetting the throbbing ache in his head, he stroked the white blaze on her forehead. Yuaneh nuzzled his arm and nickered. Tsena hugged the mare's neck, burying his face in her mane. "Oh, Yuaneh, I thought I would never see you again."

For a moment no one spoke or moved. Even Yuaneh scarcely seemed to breathe. Then Tsena heard the doctor talking to Captain Redd. He heard the men and horses moving away, and when he looked, only the captain remained.

"She is a one-man horse, *verdad?*" the captain said.

"*Sí.* You give to me *quizás?*"

Captain Redd grinned. "*Quizás.*"

This tejano *is different*, thought Tsena. *Perhaps he is the friend I need.* He combed his fingers through Yuaneh's mane. There was another question on his mind. Without looking at Redd, he asked, "If ... if Comanches do not return the captives, then what? You kill us?"

The captain did not answer immediately, so Tsena glanced at him. He stood, arms folded, staring at the ground. When he looked up his face was deadly serious.

"That is not my decision, but I tell you something. *Tejanos* do not kill women and children. It is not our way."

Tsena opened his mouth, but he could not ask the question that came to him. Was he a child in the eyes of the *tejanos*—or a man?

11

Burning to Fight

Colonel Fisher had broken his leg in the fall, so
Captain Redd took command of the mission. He allowed
Tsena a kind of freedom that Colonel Fisher never would
have allowed. He let him go to the corral and take care of
Yuaneh—brush her, talk to her. Tsena even had her old
bridle rope that his grandfather had braided. Not only
that, the captain let Tsena stand on the platform above
the gate and look out over the wall for his mother to
return with the captives. But they did not come and did
not come.

Now only three sleeps remained until the end of the
truce. After the midday meal, Tsena stood on the platform and gazed across the rolling hills toward the north-

93

west. At the opposite end of the platform two soldiers who were on watch talked between themselves.

It was a warm day for the Moon of New Grass. Tall, white clouds drifted overhead, and soldiers lounged in the shade around the square. The women and children and old Napawat dozed in their rooms. All was quiet except for the two soldiers talking now and then. The warm sun made Tsena feel drowsy too. He leaned on the top of the wall, propped his chin in his hands, and closed his eyes.

Gradually, he became aware of a low rumble. Shielding his eyes from the sun, he searched the horizon. And he listened. The rumbling grew louder. Yes, it was the sound of hooves pounding the ground—many hooves. Could it be the *Nemena*, bringing the captives to trade? Suddenly, he was wide awake.

"What do you see?" asked one of the soldiers in Spanish.

"Not see—hear," Tsena answered. "I hear many horses—maybe Comanches." He pointed to the northwest.

The two soldiers looked in that direction. One drew a pistol and held it up toward the sky.

A long, dark line appeared on the crest of a hill and spilled over it like a wave of water coming toward the mission—a wave of warriors, their spearheads glinting in the sunlight. Tsena's heart began to pound. This was no trading party!

The soldier fired his pistol into the air three times. Around the square, men stopped whatever they were doing—stopped talking, stopped polishing their guns. Others appeared at their doors. Then all at once they were shouting, running toward the gate.

Captain Redd, the first up the ladder, came and stood beside Tsena.

"Your people?" he asked.

"*Sí.*"

"Come to fight?"

"They come for us," Tsena said, hoping it was the truth.

All along the west wall soldiers climbed onto the roof of the wall lodges and knelt behind the top of the wall, their guns ready.

The warriors came on, whooping, raising their lances and bows on high. At a signal from the leader they halted some twenty paces away, making a line four or five men deep from one end of the wall to the other. *There must be three hundred of them*, Tsena guessed, but his heart plunged, for the leader of this war party was Chief Isimanica. His body glistened with bear grease and his chest jiggled like a woman's. Yet he was no woman. He was, as he said himself, a bad Indian.

Isimanica shouted in Spanish. "Come out and fight!"

Captain Redd gave orders to his men. Then, with his hands on his hips, his gun still slung over his shoulder, he faced Isimanica and said, "*Tres más días.* Three more days. We made a truce of twelve days with your people. We honor that truce."

"You lie," screamed the chief. "*Tejanos* do not have honor. You broke the truce—you took prisoners at the peace council."

"No, Comanches broke the truce," said the captain. "You did not bring all the white captives. Now we have thirty of your women and children and one old man. We want to trade."

Isimanica talked with those around him. Tsena knew he did not come to trade captives. He came for blood.

The captain turned to Tsena. "Speak to him. Tell him the only way to get his people back is to bring the captives."

Captain Redd did not know Isimanica or that he cared nothing for the women and children and one old man. Still, for the captain and for himself, Tsena would try to persuade the chief.

"Hear me, Chief Isimanica," he shouted. "My heart soared when I saw you here to rescue us. But first you must return the white captives. Did my mother not bring you the message?"

"She told us how our chiefs were massacred," Isimanica answered.

"Did she not tell you about the trade?"

"Trade?" he spat the word out as if it were bitter. "We do not come to trade. We are not women. Tell your white friend we come for blood—blood for the death of our chiefs."

"But they will kill us if you do not bring in the captives."

"No," Isimanica said, "they do not dare—they are cowards." He pranced his horse closer and swept his arm from one side to the other. "*Tejanos* hide behind walls— like women. You are cowards!" he screamed in Spanish.

The soldiers began to grumble. A few shouted angry words. Guns were cocked.

Scowling, the captain walked along the platform, speaking to them in a strong but calm voice. No one moved. He took a gun away from one of the men and motioned him down the ladder. Then he turned back to Isimanica. "I tell my men not to shoot," he said, "but they burn to fight. Return after three days and we give you a fight."

The chiefs talked among themselves. Finally, Isimanica raised his lance high and shouted, "We return."

With that they galloped away, yipping and yelling.

Tsena's heart lay on the ground.

12

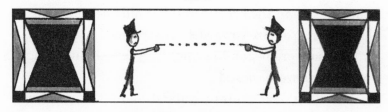

The Duel

Late that night the Thunderbird flew over the mission. He opened and closed his eyes to make flashes of lightning. He flapped his huge wings to make thunder. Then he emptied the lake he carried on his back, and rain drummed on the flat roof, pouring out of spouts.

Tsena could not understand why white man made flat roofs that did not shed rain. And he did not like sleeping in a square room. There is no power in a square, only in a circle. He longed to be safe within the circle of his own lodge.

Across the room Napawat snored. He was so old he no longer cared what happened. But Tsena lay awake thinking of Isimanica's words. *We return.* Did he mean to fight? Or would he bring some captives?

98

Outside he heard the sound of footsteps splashing through the water, then a soft knock on the door. He scrambled up from bed and opened it. A soldier stood in the doorway, holding a captive flame.

"Captain Redd says you come," he whispered.

"*Ahora?*" Tsena asked. Did the *tejanos* have no sense? It would make the Thunderbird even angrier to see him outside.

"*Sí, ahora,* now." The soldier handed him a coat and hat like the one he was wearing. "The captain says you wear."

Tsena slipped them on, wondering why Captain Redd would send for him in the middle of the night.

As they hurried across the square, Tsena could have passed for another soldier. Maybe that was the captain's idea. Suddenly, a *crack* of lightning ripped the air with a flash and stopped him in his tracks. His skin prickled.

"O mighty Thunderbird, forgive me for coming out. I have to do as the foolish *tejanos* wish."

"*Adelante,*" ordered the soldier, and Tsena hurried on. Anything to get inside.

At a knock, Captain Redd immediately opened the door.

"Enter, boy," he said. His eyes glittered.

Tsena glanced about the room. A young, dark-haired woman sat in a chair with her back to them, her face in her hands. Something was terribly wrong here. But what did it have to do with him?

"I sent for you because tomorrow I fight a duel."

"Duel?" Tsena asked. "What means duel?"

"It means two men shoot at each other."

"You fight with Comanche?"

The captain shook his head. "No, with Colonel Wells—at dawn outside the south wall. He says I am a coward for not fighting the Comanches today."

"No," Tsena protested. "You keep your word."

"Still," Captain Redd went on, "I cannot let him say that." He looked at the woman, then back at Tsena.

"If I die ..."

The woman jumped up, wrapped her arms around him, and cried, "No, William!" She looked small and childlike beside the tall captain.

He put his hand on her head and went on. "If I die, you are in danger. Not the women and children—only you. If your people do not return the captives, Colonel Wells may take revenge on you." Captain Redd paused and glanced down at the woman.

Thunder rumbled in the distance. *So it is true*, thought Tsena. *In the eyes of the* tejanos *I am a man.*

"But if I live, I try ... how do you say ... to change his mind."

Tsena looked at him in disbelief. This white man cared—actually cared—whether he lived or died. Certainly, Tsena did not want Captain Redd to die. His own life depended on it now. But what could he do?

The eagle feather ... of course! It could protect the captain from bullets—if he believed in its power.

Pulling the feather from his scalp lock he said, "I give to you. The feather of an eagle has power."

Captain Redd smiled. "*Gracias*," he said, taking the feather, but Tsena could see that he did not believe.

The woman let go of the captain then and with a sob hurried from the room.

Captain Redd reached out his hand to Tsena. "Tell nothing of what I said tonight."

Tsena took his hand in white man's way.

"*Adios*, my young friend, and good luck," the captain said.

Tsena stood, not knowing what to say or do. When the captain let go of his hand, Tsena turned to leave. At the door he stopped.

"The power of the eagle goes with you."

The captain nodded.

Once again Tsena was out in the rain. It fell softly now, and the Thunderbird no longer hovered overhead. As the soldier escorted him back to his quarters, thoughts crowded upon each other. Perhaps his own belief in the power of the eagle feather could save Captain Redd.

Yes, that was it—he must see the duel with his own eyes. But how? The captain had said *outside the walls*.

The soldier stopped at Tsena's door and waited while

he took off the coat and hat. Beside the door, water dripped into a small pool. Tsena glanced up at the water spout. Of course—from the roof!

Inside, he crept silently to his bed, felt underneath and found Yuaneh's bridle rope. He tied some knots in it and made a loop at one end. Then he lay down with the rope in hand.

It seemed he had scarcely fallen asleep when a screech owl awakened him. He sat up and opened the shutter a crack. The rain had stopped, and even though it was dark Tsena sensed that the creatures were holding their breath for the coming of Father Sun.

He got up and stood at the door waiting for the patrol. After they passed, he stepped out and tossed the loop up at the rain spout. It missed. Again he tried, and this time the loop caught. Tsena pulled it tight and began to climb with his hands. With his feet he found a knot.

A light bobbed in the far corner of the square. The next patrol! His heart lurched. He pulled himself up, up, and grabbed hold of the rain spout. He hung there for a moment, feeling for a toe hold on the stone wall, and found one at last. He pulled and pushed until he had the spout under his stomach. Steadying himself on the wall, he got a leg over the spout, then the other. The soldiers were close now. If he moved, they would notice him. So he sat on the spout, gathered up the rope, and held his breath.

They stopped directly below, took out squares of paper and tobacco, and rolled cigarettes. If they looked up now, if he made a sound ...

But the soldiers were intent on having a smoke. They held the captive flame close to their faces and began to puff. When the cigarettes were lighted they walked on, talking.

Tsena let out his breath. He climbed over the top of the wall and lay on the flat roof. His heart seemed to rock his whole body.

Presently, from the direction of the corral, he heard horses coming. In the dim light he saw two mounted men headed across the square toward the south gate. He recognized Captain Redd's tall form in the saddle.

Guards lifted the bolt and pulled the gates open. Crouching, Tsena ran along the roof to the corner of the wall. He peered over the top and watched the men ride out a short distance and dismount.

At the sound of other horses, Redd turned to face them. Tsena watched as three men rounded the corner of the mission wall. The one in the center sat erect on a sleek black horse with a silver-trimmed saddle and bridle that glittered even in the first light. *Colonel Wells*, Tsena thought, and felt his stomach twist, for this man had strong medicine. Was it stronger than the power of the eagle feather?

The men greeted one another stiffly and began to examine the guns they had brought in cases. Tsena shivered. He wrapped his arms around himself to stop the shaking.

As he watched, three of the men moved away, leaving the captain and Colonel Wells alone, standing back to back. Each held a short gun in his hand pointed at the ground. One of the three men began to bark out words—counting, it seemed. And with that, Redd and Wells stepped away from each other in time to the count—Redd with his long, loose stride, Wells stiff and erect.

O, mighty eagle, show the power of your feather, Tsena prayed.

The man pulled a white cloth from his pocket, held it high in the air, and stopped counting. Then he let it drop. Immediately, Captain Redd and Colonel Wells spun around, took aim, and fired. Birds flapped out of nearby trees.

Tsena leaped to his feet. The captain fell back, blood spurting from his head, and lay still. Colonel Wells moaned and clutched his stomach as he slumped.

Captain Redd's friend ran to him and pressed a cloth to his wound. He listened for a heartbeat. At last he stood up and shook his head. The captain was dead.

Inside the mission soldiers ran toward the gate. Tsena crouched over and headed back along the roof. From up here he could see the distant hills. Somewhere beyond them was home. He dropped down on his knees, crawled close to the outer wall, and looked over. It was a long way to the ground, but with his rope tied to the water spout, he could escape.

And leave Anawakeo and Napawat here in the mission? He pulled back from the edge. In all the confusion, no one noticed as he let himself down beside his room and stepped inside the door.

End of the Truce

Two more sleeps passed, and on the third a soldier came to Tsena's door.

"Colonel Fisher says you come," he said in Spanish.

Tsena felt a stab of alarm. The time of the truce was over—and still no captives.

He glanced back at Napawat.

"Remember not to raise your chin, Young One, or you may lose that noble nose of yours." He chuckled to himself.

How can he joke at a time like this?

"I may lose more than that," Tsena shot back. Then he strode out the door and followed the soldier across the square.

Colonel Fisher sat behind a heavy carved table with his leg propped on a stool. His blue coat was buttoned up to the collar, his mouth pressed into a thin line. *A cruel mouth*, thought Tsena.

"The squaw returns," Colonel Fisher said abruptly.

Tsena was so startled that the word did not anger him. "My mother is here?"

"In Béxar with Chief Piava." The colonel paused, watching Tsena closely. "He says he has many captives to trade. But I sent my scouts to the camp. They said there are many Comanches, but not many captives."

Tsena said nothing. He knew Chief Piava. Father had never approved of him because he spoke with a forked tongue. Was he playing some kind of trick now?

"You know this chief?" the colonel asked.

Tsena nodded.

"You have nothing to say, boy?"

"What you want of me?"

He lunged forward and banged his fist on the table. "The truth! Does Piava tell the truth?"

Tsena kept his face blank. "I do not know," he answered.

The colonel stared at him. The pupils of his blue eyes were like needle points trying to pierce his mind.

At last he leaned back. "Very well. Tomorrow I send Captain Howard to meet with Piava. He takes you and eight other prisoners. You choose them. *Comprende?*"

"*Sí, comprendo.*" But he understood nothing. Not

what would happen tomorrow or what Chief Piava had planned.

In the morning the soldiers swung the main gate open, and Tsena and eight other prisoners rode out in a wagon pulled by a team of horses. On either side of them were mounted soldiers, led by Captain Howard. He looked soft and plump to Tsena, not like a soldier. His dark curls bounced as his horse trotted. The prairie dog interpreter rode at his side.

Choosing who was to come had been difficult. Women had begged, thrusting their children into his arms. In the end he chose Anawakeo and her Grandmother Moko, two wounded women, a woman and her child of four winters, a motherless child, and Napawat.

Now, as the wagon bounced along the road to Béxar, Tsena hoped Colonel Fisher was wrong about the captives. Maybe they had been hidden from the *tejano* scouts. But try as he would to be hopeful, Tsena could not get rid of the dark suspicion that there were no captives left.

He glanced at Anawakeo, sitting on the other side of the wagon.

"Thank you for choosing Grandmother and me," she said.

Tsena nodded. Of course he would choose them. It was the others that had been difficult.

"You should have left me, boy," said Napawat. "I have little time left."

"That is why I chose you, Old One," Tsena said. He looked out across the rolling land. "You should see the meadows now—they are blooming with blue and red flowers."

Napawat took a deep breath. "Yes, I smell them, Young One. Mother Earth shows her happiness. May the spirits also be happy today."

They skirted around Béxar, and on the far side a line of mounted warriors awaited them, each with his bow or lance in hand. As the wagon drew closer, Tsena saw Chief Piava at the center, his wiry body in full war paint. Behind him, mounted on the horse the *tejanos* had given her, was Topay. She stared at Tsena without expression.

Captain Howard called a halt at ten or twelve paces away. Soldiers spread out on either side of him, their guns ready. Then he spoke, and his words were repeated by the interpreter.

"Where are the captives?"

Chief Piava looked at the *tejano* soldiers. His mouth was like an angry scar across his face. It opened. "We have two captives to exchange for two of yours."

Two? thought Tsena, his hopes plummeting. *Why only two?*

The chief motioned, and from behind the warriors, two children were brought forward—a small white girl and a *mexicano* boy. The girl had burn scars on her face. She hung back.

The captain turned to look at the wagon. In spite of

his soft, round face, his eyes were hard. He pointed at Anawakeo.

"You, girl, and that child," said the interpreter.

She arose and shook her head. "No, not without . . ." She glanced at Tsena . . . "not without the others."

The pleasure of her words spread through his body, but he did not let it show on his face as he stood.

"Your grandfather would want you to go—and I speak for him here."

She looked startled. Then she tilted her head to one side, seeming to ask, *Will we ever see each other again?*

He wanted to take her by the shoulders and say, *I swear by Father Sun and Mother Earth . . . we shall.*

She seemed to understand what he was thinking and turned to embrace her grandmother.

"Go quickly, my child, before they change their minds," Moko said.

Anawakeo climbed down from the wagon and held her arms out for the small boy. He went with her willingly across the empty space to the other side.

The white girl did not come so willingly. She struggled to pull away from the soldier who brought her to the wagon and set her in it.

"I want my mother," she bawled, looking back at the *Nemena*.

"Hush now," Moko said to her. "*Nemena* children do not cry."

110

The girl looked at Moko, her mouth turned down, her chin trembling, but she became quiet.

Then Captain Howard spoke to the interpreter. "Why have you not brought in *all* the captives?" he demanded.

Tsena watched Chief Piava closely. His small eyes revealed nothing, his mouth remained tightly shut.

Captain Howard, his anger barely contained by the high stiff collar of his jacket, repeated the question.

Still the chief sat stonily silent.

The captain shifted in his saddle. He blew out through his mouth and turned stiffly to glance at his men on either side. Horses stomped their hooves and swished their tails.

"Do you have any more captives?" he asked, more reasonably.

The chief straightened himself. "We have only one white boy back in our camp. If we give him up, I will choose for myself which one of our people we take."

What is he up to? Tsena wondered. *First he said they had only two captives, but now they have another.*

Captain Howard took his time in answering. When he spoke, his voice was low and commanding.

"Agreed," said the interpreter, seeming relieved at the word. "Meet us here in the morning with the boy."

Anawakeo had mounted behind Topay. The two of them watched silently as the wagon carrying Tsena, Moko, and the others turned and headed back to Béxar.

The next morning Tsena and six other prisoners made the trip in the wagon again, led by Captain Howard. The *Nemena* were again waiting. Piava had the boy with him on his horse. He peered around the chief at the *tejanos*. His head had been shaved and his body painted, but there were no marks of torture. He was about eleven winters old, Tsena imagined.

Anawakeo and Topay, mounted on separate horses that morning, were directly behind Piava. As the chief studied the captives in the wagon, Topay moved up beside him and spoke.

"I ask you, Piava, choose my son."

The chief did not answer. Already he seemed to have forgotten that she was the wife of a great chief. Instead he pointed at Anawakeo's grandmother. "I take Moko."

"*Och*, no," she said, shaking her jowels. "Choose another. I am too old."

"Grandmother!" Anawakeo blurted, but immediately clapped her hand over her mouth.

The chief then addressed himself to Captain Howard. The serene countenance vanished. His face contorted with anger. "She is my choice. Bring her forward, I say!"

Now it was Captain Howard's turn to remain unmoved.

"Why do you choose her?" the interpreter asked.

Piava eyed the captain for a moment. Then he smiled and said, "I want her for my wife. She has many horses."

When Captain Howard understood the words, he reared back and laughed. "The lady says no, Piava."

The smile on the chief's face faded to a scowl. "You *tejanos* are not men. You let women tell you what to do."

Howard stiffened. Then he spoke slowly, spacing his words and keeping his eyes on Piava.

The interpreter opened his mouth but said nothing. He looked ready to dive for his hole again. Whatever Captain Howard had said, the interpreter was not going to translate this time. Soldiers muttered among themselves. Some raised their guns. Warriors nocked arrows. Tsena felt as if they stood on either side of a ravine, and one loose rock—or word—could send them hurtling to the bottom.

The chief pranced his horse back and forth with the white boy holding to his waist. Suddenly, he pulled up short, facing Howard, and pointed at the wagon.

"The young one," he yelled.

Captain Howard kept his mouth clamped shut.

Slowly the woman stood, holding her boy-child by the hand. She said nothing, only nodded, and climbed down from the wagon to lead the child to Piava. He turned away and spoke to the white boy behind him. The boy dismounted and looked uncertain for a moment until Captain Howard motioned for him to come.

Piava reached down for the woman's child, but he shrank toward his mother. She whispered in his ear and lifted him to the chief, who gently set the child in front of him.

"You ride the chief's horse," he said.

A grin spread across the child's face.

Slowly guns were lowered and bowstrings released. All eyes were on the child. Tsena felt himself smiling and looked around. The boy's expression had spread to almost all faces—except for old Napawat.

"The boy likes his new father," Tsena told him.

Napawat nodded, but he did not smile.

Captain Howard looked around at them and spoke some words.

"You, old man. You go too," said the interpreter.

Tsena hesitated. He had not expected this.

As he helped Napawat down from the wagon, the old man whispered, "They are dead, Young One. All the other white captives are dead. You must make your escape tonight."

14

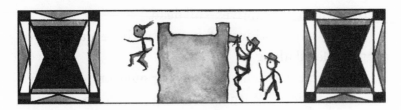

Leap into Darkness

Captain Howard led the soldiers and prisoners back into Béxar with the white boy riding behind him. The boy's excited voice drifted back to Tsena, but he could not understand the words. Was Napawat right? Was the boy telling him that all the captives were dead?

In the square Captain Howard called a halt. People were gathered outside the council lodge—both *tejanos* and *mexicanos*. Men crowded around the captain. One of them helped the boy down and led him through the doorway.

No one spoke on the ride back to the mission. The only sounds were the clomp of hooves, the creak of the wagon. The late afternoon sky had grown overcast and mist had begun to fall.

Good, thought Tsena. *It will be a dark night.*

When they arrived back inside the mission, Captain Howard dismounted and came around to the wagon. Tsena climbed down and stood waiting, not knowing what to expect.

Captain Howard's face was grim. "The boy says there are no more captives—all dead."

Tsena said nothing. It was a truth he had known deep inside all along.

"You and the women go to your quarters. Do not go out. *Comprende?*" Without waiting for an answer, the captain turned on his heel and stalked toward Colonel Fisher's quarters.

Tsena's small room seemed lonely without Napawat sitting by the fire pit. He wished the old man were here to listen to his plan for escape. Still, what was there to discuss? There was only one way out of the mission— over the wall.

He reached under his bed to make sure the rope was still there. It was. Should he tell Anawakeo's grandmother? Yes, he decided, but not now—after dark.

Tsena stepped to the doorway and looked out at the light rain falling. No one was about, only the patrols. As one pair approached, he shrank back into the room.

After they passed by, Moko suddenly appeared at his door, clutching a blanket around her short, plump figure.

He motioned her inside. "You take a risk, Grandmother," he said respectfully.

116

"I am not afraid, my boy. They will not harm the women and children—I believe your Captain Redd. They will let us go by the end of this moon, I think." She paused. "But I fear for you."

Tsena dipped his head to her. "I . . . I have a plan for escape," he said, closing the door.

"Tell me," she said, looking closely at him. Her round face was remarkably unlined, Tsena noticed.

"I have a rope," he began. "Late tonight I will use it to go over the wall. Then I will make my way around to the other side where the horses are put out to graze. In the morning I will take Yuaneh from them."

She nodded slowly. "It is good." She put a hand on his shoulder. "So, I say farewell. May our paths soon cross again." She started for the door.

There was something more he wanted to say to her, but he could not think how.

"With all my heart I wish it too, Grandmother."

She looked around at him from the corners of her eyes. "You cannot be so anxious to see an old woman. Is there someone else you wish to see?"

Tsena felt his face flush. Glancing down at his moccasins he said, "It is your granddaughter. Tell her . . ." He looked up then. ". . . I will not forget."

She smiled. "I will tell her."

Just before sunset two soldiers brought pans of corn bread and dried beef, and left them in the doorways. After eating, Tsena stuck the rest of the beef inside his

117

belt. Then he reached up to the crack over the window, pulled out the gun barrel, and tied it to the fringe of his leggings.

At last darkness came. With his rope in hand he waited beside the doorway until the patrol passed. One of them carried a captive flame. As the light faded away, Tsena stepped out and threw the loop up toward the rain spout. It fell back to the ground. He could not see the spout, but he knew where it was. Again he tossed the rope, and again it fell back to him.

Soon the other patrol would be coming. His hands shook as he enlarged the loop. Taking a deep breath, he looked up and threw the rope. This time it caught.

Hand over hand Tsena climbed, gripping with his feet. He pulled himself up on the rain spout. Without pause he crawled over the wall, onto the roof, and lay there, panting. His pulse throbbed in his ears. The patrol approached, their light bobbing. But instead of walking by, they stopped just below him.

The rope! It still hung from the rain spout.

The soldiers shouted, and Tsena could hear one of them grunting as he started up the rope.

His heart pounded like a stone hammer as he crept to the other side of the wall and looked over the edge into blackness. He had to jump. Any moment they would be on the roof. He sat on the edge and pushed off, his arms spread like wings. When he struck the ground, his ankle turned sharply under him, and he heard a *pop*.

More shouting, this time from outside the wall.

Tsena scrambled up and started to run. Pain shot up his leg. He staggered, fell, crawled on. From behind came the heavy stomp of boots crashing through the underbrush.

Up again, limping, fighting forward. Dark trees loomed, the ground dropped away. He fell, rolling over rocks, down an embankment. Quickly he crawled to a tree and crouched among the roots on the bank.

Rain fell heavily now, and his buckskin shirt clung to his back and arms as he waited, scarcely breathing. Soldiers were all around. One of them held up a captive flame. It made a circle of yellow light streaked with rain. The others thrashed about among the bushes, now and then calling to the man with the light.

Tsena froze as one of them strode closer. The man stopped beside the tree and poked about with his gun in the underbrush. Tsena clenched his muscles and made his body as hard as the roots. The barrel jabbed his leg, but he made no sound, and the soldier moved on.

At last the men called to one another, and Tsena watched the light, surrounded by dark forms, move through the rain back toward the mission.

For a long time he lay shivering in his wet clothes. His ankle throbbed. Then holding to the tree, he stood on his right leg and put a little weight on his left. *Och,* the pain!

He let himself down and gingerly felt around his

ankle. Nothing was out of place. Then he remembered that *pop*, the *pop* of his bone, and he knew it was broken. All because he had left the rope dangling. How could he have been so stupid? He sat in the rain. His plan was ruined. The soldiers would be back in the morning to find him.

So, with no plan in mind, Tsena crawled down the muddy bank, through the creek and up the other side. Underbrush scratched his face and tore at his hair.

When he came to a grassy place, he stopped to rest. His hands were sore and bleeding, but he had to keep moving, had to get farther from the mission.

Then an idea came to him. He slipped off his moccasins and put them on his hands. He crawled across the meadow this way, into a stand of trees, on and on. In the darkness the throbbing of his ankle was all he knew. His arms and legs moved themselves through the wet grass, over rocks and fallen trees—like one of the four-legged creatures.

Gradually he became aware of a roar, and then he was slipping, sliding down a muddy bank into rushing water. It caught him, and carried him along. The water drew him under, and filled his nostrils. He fought upward for air and gasped a breath, stroking toward the shore. But the water had its way, swirling him, hurling him into rocks. A branch raked across his face. He grabbed hold and clung to it with both hands. The current pulled, trying to take him.

He tightened his grip with one hand, and reached higher on the branch with the other. Then, hand over hand, he slowly pulled himself out of the raging creek until he was hanging over the bank. Dangling by one arm he pulled his left knee up to his chest and let go. He landed on his good leg and slid back down to the water's edge. His arms trembled as he clawed his way up the muddy bank.

At the top Tsena collapsed and lay on his back. If the creek wanted to come up and take him it could. He had nothing left—no strength, no hope. His throat tightened and he could not hold back. He began to cry.

Everything was ruined. The spirits had turned away from him. He would die here.

15

The Wolf

But he did not die. The ache in his ankle awoke him, and he eased over on his back. He looked up into the liveoak branches silhouetted against the first light of day.

How could he have made such a mess of his escape? Even now he could be lying in wait for Yuaneh to be turned out. What was he to do?

Clouds in the east turned pink and then slowly into glowing red coals. Night was over, the rain was over. Tsena felt a sudden rush of hope—for no good reason except that Father Sun was returning. He sat up, pulled off his shirt, and watched the top of the rise across the river.

At the first flash of rays, he lifted his arms. "Father Sun, let your power enter my body so that I can do what I need to do." He sat still for a time, feeling warm strength seep into his body.

Then he looked down at his ankle. It was beginning to swell. He ripped a seam in one side of his leggings and pulled it up.

"First I need a splint."

Talking aloud made him feel better, as if he were not alone. By the river he saw some sticks that had washed up. He crawled down and brought them back to his place under the liveoak. Then he tore off a length of creeper vine growing on the trunk. As he held two sticks against his leg and wrapped the vine around them, he remembered how he had cried the night before—cried like a child—and he flushed with shame.

When his ankle was bound, Tsena began planning what to do. "I have water to drink. I will stay here until my leg heals and then go back for Yuaneh. But what will I eat?" His stomach gnawed as he thought of the beef. It was gone, probably carried away by the river. Fortunately the river did not take the barrel coup. It was still safely tied to his leggings.

He looked around at the rocks lying on the ground. He could gather them and make a slingshot to kill a squirrel or rabbit. Crawling about, he tossed rocks onto a pile.

He continued talking to himself as he made a crude

sling out of a scrap of buckskin and fringe torn from his leggings.

"Now I sit and wait."

Presently he saw a hawk circling above. On the ground below, a rabbit crouched like a gray stone in the meadow. Tsena placed a rock in the strap and slowly got up on his knees. Then, whirling the sling around and around over his head, he let go of one end. The rock flew, landing in the grass just short of his target. The rabbit leaped up and began hopping away. Like an arrow the hawk dived, clutched the rabbit in his talons, flapped his wings, and took off.

Tsena sighed. Without his bow it was going to be difficult to make a kill. A person could go for several sleeps without eating, he knew, but no one could last for long. He would have to kill something.

"What if I cannot?" he asked himself. "But I *will* kill something."

When the sun stood at the zenith and he had not made a kill, he crawled down to the water's edge and drank. The river flowed calmly now that it was shrunk back to its bed. He stripped off his clothes and let himself into the water. It soothed his swollen ankle. After a while he rinsed the mud from his shirt, leggings, and moccasins, and placed them on a rock to dry. The warm sun made him drowsy, and he slept.

It had sunk halfway down the sky by the time he awoke and saw a squirrel flicking his tail and scolding from a branch overhead. He took up his sling, but again he missed.

At sunset Tsena prayed for help. If only he had a guardian spirit to hear him, to give him power. Darkness came on and he stretched out, looking up at the vast meadow of stars.

"Tomorrow," he said. "Tomorrow I will kill something." But he did not sound as sure.

The next day a deer came to the river upwind. In his mind Tsena nocked an arrow, pulled the string back, and sent the arrow flying straight to the heart. He ran to the deer, cut out the liver, and ate it while it was still warm and steaming. He ran his tongue between his lips, thinking of the salty taste.

But the deer drank peacefully, occasionally lifting his head to look for danger.

Once again darkness came, and stars began to sparkle. Tsena lay back and looked in the northern sky for the Star That Does Not Walk Around. He could be riding home on Yuaneh now, guided by that star.

Suddenly angry with himself, he sat up. He picked up a rock and threw it into the river, and another and another until he used them all.

Two more sleeps passed without a kill. All the creatures knew of his presence and stayed away. He tightened the splint as swelling in his ankle began to go down. And he prayed to the spirits.

His stomach was silent now—he craved only water.

As he crawled toward the river for a drink, the trees seemed to swirl around him, and he lay down until the feeling passed.

That night the howling of a wolf awoke Tsena. He opened his eyes and sat up. The bitten moon was rising, and out of its bitten edge leaped a white wolf. It galloped along the moon path toward him, growing brighter and brighter. Tsena stared with a chill of awe.

The wolf stopped at the edge of the spreading live-oak branches and stood looking at him with his yellow eyes.

"Rise up, Tsena Naku, He Who Hears the Wolf."

Tsena rose up on his knees. For a moment he felt himself reeling and thought he would fall down. But he fastened his gaze on the wolf's shining eyes and held himself steady. Was he dreaming, or was this a vision?

"Do not be afraid, for behold, I am Spirit Wolf. I bring you my power—the power to withstand bullets and to see what will be."

Tsena caught his breath.

"Tomorrow my messenger will come and end your fast. At dawn go and bathe in the river. Then sit under this tree and face the rising sun. When it strikes your face, you must sing this song." The wolf lifted his muzzle and sang.

"The white wolves come running,
The white wolves come running.

Behold them and listen,
Behold them and speak."

He looked at Tsena. "Always remember your song. Sing it when you need my power."

Tsena nodded. "I will do so, Spirit Wolf."

The wolf said no more, but he stayed for a time looking at Tsena with his shining eyes, and Tsena at him. Then the wolf shook his white fur, turned, and galloped back up the moon path. He stopped once for another look back before disappearing into the brightness of the moon.

Tsena dropped down on all fours and crawled to the spot where the wolf had stood. He found a tuft of fur, a stone his paw had turned, and some grass he had flattened. He opened his medicine bag and put these things in it. At last he had medicine. He had power. For a long while he sat staring at the bitten moon. Then he lay down and slept.

At first light Tsena awoke and crawled down to the river as Spirit Wolf had instructed him. After stripping off his leggings, he tightened the splint. His ankle was not as swollen now. Then he untied his breechcloth and eased himself into the water. He stayed near the shallow edge, for in his weakness the river could carry him away. For a time he lay there, letting the water wash over him and marveling at his shining vision.

As Tsena crawled back up the bank he had to stop

and rest, for his arms threatened to fold under him. When he reached the tree he sat facing east.

The moment Father Sun peeked over the rise across the river, Tsena raised his arms and began his song.

> "*The white wolves come running,*
> *The white wolves come running.*
> *Behold them and listen,*
> *Behold them and speak.*"

Four times he sang it and then sat with his eyes closed, letting the rays enter his body.

"*Hola!*" came a voice from upstream.

Tsena jerked his head around and grabbed a rock. There, mounted on a yellow horse, was a boy with yellow hair. He had a long gun strapped over his shoulder. *How did he get so close without a sound?* Tsena wondered. He clutched the rock. If the boy took up his gun, he would get it on the head.

"You came from the mission?" the boy asked in Spanish.

Tsena did not answer. He turned the smooth, rounded rock over and over with his fingers.

"Your leg is broken?" he went on.

The two looked at each other in silence. He was about his own age, Tsena imagined. Overhead a mocking-bird sang.

Slowly the boy dismounted. "I do not shoot if you do not throw the rock."

Tsena gripped the rock. He would not lay it down no matter what this *tejano* said. It was a trick.

"My father is a doctor in Béxar." He glanced at Tsena's splint. "He can help you. We do not tell the soldiers."

A doctor? Could he be the one who had come to the mission?

Tsena studied the boy's face. He had a pointed chin and sharp features that gave him the look of a fox. His brown eyes were keen. It was an intelligent face—even friendly.

"You have hunger?" the boy asked then.

Tsena caught his breath. *My messenger will end your fast*, Spirit Wolf had said. This yellow-haired boy was the wolf's messenger! He let the rock fall to the ground and nodded.

The boy walked back to his horse and returned with a stick of bread. "I have only corn bread."

Tsena nodded his thanks. He took a small bite, chewed slowly, and swallowed. It was enough—he could not eat more.

"I am called Will," the boy said, "Will Smithers. My father is Doctor Smithers. You know?"

At last Tsena spoke. "*Sí* . . . I think so. He came to the mission when Colonel Fisher broke his leg, *verdad?*"

"*Sí, verdad.*"

"He—how do you say—he helped me when a soldier hit me with his gun." Tsena pointed to his temple.

Will nodded. "My father told me. He said you were a tall thin boy, son of a chief."

"I am called Tsena," he said. "It means wolf."

"Wolf?" Will's eyebrows went up. "How strange! I saw a white wolf this morning and followed him here. Then he disappeared into the woods."

There was a long silence. Will seemed to be trying to understand. But Tsena could not tell him about his vision or the power might be lost.

In a moment Will said, "You broke your leg when you left the mission?"

"*Sí*, I jumped from the wall because Colonel Fisher wants to kill me."

Will nodded. "Come to my *casa* in town. We give you food and a bed until your leg is *bueno*. Nobody sees you there. You like?"

"I like, but we wait for dark."

"*Bueno*," Will said. "I have a plan." He pointed toward town. "We go to the place where the river turns. You hide there. Tonight my father and I return, and we go to my *casa*."

Tsena smiled. It was a good plan. The wolf had chosen his messenger wisely.

1⟨ꞌ

Casa of the Doctor

As Father Sun sank behind the hills Tsena saw two riders in the distance. He crawled behind the cottonwood tree and watched as they came closer. One was riding a yellow horse with black mane and tail. Yes, it was Will, and the one on the black horse must be his father. Tsena moved from behind the tree and raised his arm to them.

At the top of the riverbank they dismounted, and Will ran down it, a small bundle in hand.

"Here is meat!" he said, handing it to Tsena.

He unwrapped it, and the smell suddenly made his hunger fierce. He tore off a piece with his teeth, chewed, swallowed, and his stomach clenched into a knot.

"Slowly, my boy, slowly," said the doctor.

Tsena took a smaller bite and chewed a long time, keeping his eyes on the next one.

Doctor Smithers knelt and looked at the splint. "You have pain now?"

Tsena shook his head. "No *más* pain." He marveled at the doctor's thick mustache. It was carefully trimmed, and the ends curled down around his mouth.

"*Bueno*," the doctor said, nodding. Then he smoothed his mustache and chuckled. "You think my mustache is very strange, eh? But we are not so different, my boy. You see, what is on one's face is not as important as what is in one's heart."

"*Es verdad*," Tsena said and smiled.

When darkness came they mounted and rode back to Béxar, Tsena behind Will on the horse he called Sandy. As they passed through the streets, Tsena looked in the glowing windows. Through one of them he glimpsed a man lifting a child over his head—just like Father used to do with Chawakeh, and never would do again.

They rode on, around a corner, along a high wall and stopped at the double door of a *casa*. Will dismounted and walked to the doors, leaving Tsena alone on the horse.

Tsena realized he could take the reins, slip into the saddle, and gallop off. They could not follow him in the dark. He could ride out of this town and across the hills to home. He reached for the reins, stopped for a moment, and drew back.

No . . . he could not offend his guardian spirit. The

wolf sent Will to help him. And in truth Tsena did not want to offend Will or the doctor.

"*Casa* for horses," Will said as he opened the doors. "We call it stable."

Tsena laughed. It was as much from relief that he did not bolt as from the thought of keeping horses in a *casa*. "I feel sorrow for the horses."

Will laughed too. Then he said, "So Comanches cannot take them."

They laughed together, although a little uneasily, it seemed to Tsena.

Inside the dark stable he let himself slide off the horse and stood on one leg, leaning against the wall. The doctor opened a door on the other side and stepped out.

"My father goes for a lantern," Will said. "We wait here."

They waited in the darkness. The only sounds were the horses snorting and shaking their bridles and Tsena's stomach growling. He hoped there would be something more to eat tonight.

Soon Doctor Smithers returned with a captive flame, or lantern as Will called it. Tsena looked around the stable. In the center stood a wagon. To the left were two pens where Will and his father led the horses and began unsaddling them.

When Will finished brushing Sandy, he came over to the wagon. "We make your bed here."

Tsena looked inside. There was a thick layer of dry grass, a blanket, and a crutch.

Will picked up the crutch and handed it to him. "So you can walk."

For a moment Tsena held it, looked at it and then at Will.

"Why do you want to help me?" Tsena asked.

"Why not?"

"Because you are *tejano* and I am *Nemena*."

"Maybe that is the reason." Will smoothed back his hair that fell across his forehead. "And because of that wolf. It seems like he led me to you." He shook his head. "I cannot understand."

If the doctor was listening to their conversation, he made no sign. He went about bringing dry grass for the horses to eat.

When the horses had been fed and watered, Doctor Smithers took Tsena by the arm. "Now, we go in the *casa*. I want to look at your leg."

With the doctor on one side and the crutch on the other, Tsena hobbled out the door.

"*Casita*," said Will, pointing to a tiny *casa* attached to the stable. "Where you go to make water."

Tsena nodded. It was like the mission. But he would never get used to white man's ways. Horses living in *casas*, people relieving themselves in *casitas*!

They walked along a stone path, through the patio toward the big *casa*. The smell of roasting meat made Tsena's mouth water.

Will pointed to the right. "*Casa* for cooking. I bring more food to you after my father looks at your leg."

Good, thought Tsena as he glanced around. *So many* casas—*this place is like a village.*

When the doctor opened the door of the big *casa*, tinkling music came from the other end of a passageway, and they stopped to listen.

"My little sister plays the piano," Will whispered.

Tsena did not know the word *piano*, but the slow melody she played went straight to his heart. He began to think that staying inside these walls for a few sleeps would not be so bad. As he hobbled along, Tsena glanced at the painted pictures lining the wall. A younger doctor in a black coat, a little boy that looked like Will, a rosy-cheeked woman with a baby on her lap.

The passageway opened into a long room. Tsena stopped, his eyes dazzled by so many glowing candles. The light reflected in wall mirrors and silver utensils. Red and blue rugs lay on the polished floor. At the far end of the room a girl with curly yellow hair sat at the piano making music with her fingers. The same woman as in the painted picture and a young man sat listening. No one seemed to be aware of them.

When Will's sister finished the music, she turned and gasped. The other two looked around, and for a moment they stared in silence.

Doctor Smithers spoke to them in white man's words, and then to Tsena in Spanish. "My wife, *Señora*

Smithers, my daughter Agatha, and the teacher of my children, *Señor* Peck."

They continued to stare at Tsena as if he were a wild animal who did not belong in the *casa*. He felt that way himself. The effect of the music vanished like smoke up a smoke hole, and he wanted out of this square lodge with its thick walls and staring *tejanos*. He wanted to run but knew he could not. Instead he drew a deep breath, straightened his back, and lifted his chin—which seemed to offend *Señor* Peck, for he looked away.

The doctor took Tsena's arm and helped him through a doorway and into a smaller room on the right. Will brought a candle and lighted a lamp that stood on a center table. Only when the door was closed did Tsena breathe freely.

"They have to get accustomed to the idea," said the doctor and pointed to the table. "Now sit here, my boy."

Tsena nodded, but it seemed unlikely. He watched while the doctor poured water into a basin, washed his hands, and gently unwound the vine that held the splint together. With cold, clean fingers he felt Tsena's lower leg, pressing just above the ankle bone until a sharp pain shot up his leg.

Tsena jerked.

"Sorry," Doctor Smithers said.

After a moment the doctor looked up at him. "Well, I think you broke the large bone in your leg, but if you do not walk for three weeks, it can heal. *Bueno?*"

"Three weeks?" asked Tsena. "How much time?"

"Not long," the doctor answered, "only twenty-one days."

Och, Tsena thought, *that is a long time to stay here.* Still, it would seem longer if he were sitting by the creek with nothing to eat. He had much to be thankful for.

"*Bueno*," he answered.

The doctor smiled. He took a roll of shiny metal from a cabinet and began to cut it. Will brought a pan of water and washed Tsena's leg.

"I like to help my father, because I want to be a doctor too."

Tsena nodded. "And I want to be a chief—like my father."

They were silent as Tsena watched Will wrap cloth around his leg and the doctor fit the metal splint over it. He did not feel as sure as he sounded. But he was sure of one thing now. The *Nemena* would seek blood revenge for their chiefs. Once he was back in his village, how could he, son of one of them, not do the same? How could he keep his promise to Father?

"I feel sorrow for your father," Will said, looking up at him.

It startled Tsena, and he could not think what to say, much less how to say it in Spanish. Why were these *tejanos* helping him? Why had Spirit Wolf chosen a white messenger? To confuse him?

Later that night Will brought a plate of roasted beef

and boiled potatoes out to the stable. After eating, Tsena crawled into the wagon and lay down. A full stomach put his mind at ease, at least for now. All he had to think about was going home. Once he returned to the village, he would seek an answer from the wolf.

Waking in the dim light of the stable next morning, Tsena sat up and gazed at the two horses in their pens. They stirred, and Sandy turned to look at him.

"*Mariah weh*, my friends, good morning. Do you understand *Nemena* talk?"

The doctor's black mare lifted her head and whinnied.

"Sure you do. And I understand horse talk. You want out to gallop across the meadow." He felt about in the straw, found his crutch, and let himself down from the back of the wagon. "I envy you," he went on. "You will get out today, but I have to sit around for twenty-one sleeps."

With a sigh he hobbled to the door and opened it. The rising sun was hidden by roofs. The patio was enclosed by the big *casa*, the cooking *casa*, the stable, and a wall beyond the vegetable garden. He longed to be out where the wind blew freely and there was nothing to block Father Sun.

Just then Tsena caught the smell of fat meat cooking, and the longing in his stomach made him forget all else. He settled himself under a green berry tree to wait for Will.

No sooner had he sat down than Will came striding

out the back door, his trousers tucked inside boots, his hair combed to one side.

"*Buenos días*, Tsena. You have hunger?"

"*Sí*, my nose gives me *mucho* hunger."

Will laughed and stepped into the cooking *casa*. He brought out metal plates of eggs, with strips of fat meat and little round cakes.

"Your mother cooks good food," Tsena said.

"Not my mother—Carmencita."

"Is she number two wife?"

Will threw back his head and laughed.

"I say a funny word?" Tsena asked.

"*Sí*," said Will. "I mean no. It is funny because white men never have more than one wife."

"Hmm," Tsena said. "In my village, he who has many horses has two or three wives."

"*Por favor*, I do not laugh at you—I laugh because Carmencita is our *servant*, not the wife of my father."

Tsena was puzzled. "What is *servant*?" he asked.

Will thought a moment. "It means . . . a person who does the work of the *casa*. My father pays her."

Tsena nodded. "Maybe not so different. Comanches have many wives to do work of the *casa*. White men marry only one wife and pay another to do the work. *Verdad?*"

"Something like that," Will said.

Even so, Tsena thought, *if I have Anawakeo for my wife, I will not love another.*

139

When they finished eating, Will took the plates. "I return after my lessons with *Señor* Peck." He stretched his neck high and walked away imitating his teacher. Tsena laughed heartily for the first time since his capture.

With Will gone, he had nothing to do but sit and watch the comings and goings of the family, like an old man. The doctor came and examined his splint and asked if he had slept well. Will's mother and Carmencita, a small *mexicano* woman, went to the garden to gather vegetables. When *Señor* Peck walked by to the *casita*, Tsena had to duck his head to keep from laughing again—so perfectly had Will imitated the teacher's manner.

Presently Will came out leading Agatha by the hand. "I told Agatha you do not want her scalp, but she does not believe me. Maybe you can tell her."

The little girl stayed close to her brother, one finger in her mouth, looking at Tsena from the corner of her eyes. How different she was from Chawakeh, with her sunlit hair curling around her face. And yet, the curiosity in her eyes was the same.

"I have a little sister too," Tsena began. "She is the same size as you, but she has hair the color of a blackbird."

Agatha looked at him more directly now.

"She likes to play the game of hands. Do you like to play?"

Agatha shook her head no.

Tsena picked up a small round stone, made fists with both hands, and passed the stone back and forth between them.

"Now, which hand has the stone?" he asked, thrusting out his two fists.

Agatha took her finger from her mouth and pointed to his right hand. Tsena opened his empty fist. Then he showed her the stone in his left hand.

Her blue eyes opened wider. "Again," she said quietly.

Once more Tsena moved his arms about, over his head, to one side and the other, passing the stone or pretending to pass it from hand to hand. At last he stopped and held out his fists. This time she guessed the left hand. He opened his fist, and there lay the stone.

She squealed with delight.

"Now you," Tsena said, holding the stone out to her.

She reached to take it but withdrew quickly at the touch of their hands, and the stone fell to the ground. Will picked it up for her. Clumsily she swapped it back and forth, watching her hands. She stopped and held out her small fists. Tsena knew very well which one held the stone, so he pointed to the other. Her face shone with pleasure as she showed him her empty hand.

Slowly the days went by, and Tsena's leg grew stronger. He imagined himself riding Yuaneh across the hills to his village. Even if they had moved he could find it, for they always stayed near Lone Hill.

Occasionally he forgot about going home when he was playing games with Agatha or talking with Will. Or when Carmencita brought him a plate of small cakes and milk. "To make strong bones," she said.

One sunny afternoon Tsena, Will, and Agatha sat together under the green berry tree. Tsena braided a horsehair bridle for Yuaneh while Agatha sat on the wooden bench and drew on her slate. Beside her, Will peered through the round pieces of glass he wore over his eyes, reading signs in a book. *Spectacles* he called them, and said he could not read without them.

Tsena wondered about white man's signs. How could they be so interesting? Sometimes Will frowned as his eyes moved back and forth. Sometimes he laughed out loud. But most amazing were those times when he was so engrossed that he did not hear anyone speak to him.

"Can you show me how to read signs?" Tsena asked him.

Will kept on reading until Agatha laid down her slate and poked him. He looked up, surprised, and Tsena repeated the question.

Will thought a moment and picked up Agatha's book. Opening to the first page, he turned it to face Tsena. There were two pictures of a dog. The signs were much larger than in Will's book.

"Here, this word is *dog*. It means *perro*. *Comprende?*"

Tsena nodded. "*Dog–uh*," he repeated.

"Look at the word. Can you find another one like it?"

He looked closely at the word as he would look at an animal track. There were three circles—the first one had a stem pointing up, the middle one was plain, and the third had a curling tail. Once he had the pattern in mind he looked below and found the same track.

"Here! This one says *dog–uh* too."

"*Sí*, very good."

Agatha picked up her slate. "I can teach you how to write your name. You like?" Her eyes were bright with excitement.

"*Sí*, I like."

She put the piece of chalk to the slate and hesitated, frowning. Then Will told her what to write, sign by sign.

"Tsena," she said when she finished. Turning the slate to him she named the signs, pointing to each. "*T-S-E-N-A*. Now you write."

He held the slate in one hand, and with a stick in the other began to copy the signs in the dirt. They were not as neat and straight as Agatha's, and the *E* was too big.

Day by day he learned to write other signs—of her name, Will's, and of some white man words like *BOY* and *HORSE* and *FRIEND*.

"You learn fast," Will said.

Tsena felt his heart swell for he knew it was true. Given enough time, he too could sit absorbed in signs like Will. But there was not much time. Once his leg healed he and Yuaneh would ride away, never to return.

He thought often about his plan to steal Yuaneh, but

he told no one. Sometimes when he was helping Will brush the horses he talked about him—how Yuaneh was his best friend, and how Captain Redd had brought her to the mission. Balanced on his crutch, he would comb out the tangles in Sandy's black mane and pretend that the horse was Yuaneh.

"But how can you go back without her?" Will asked once as he worked on the opposite side of the horse.

Tsena went on brushing, but he said nothing.

Will ducked under the horse's neck, his eyes wide. "You are *not* going back without her!"

Tsena shook his head. "No."

"Then I want to help you."

17

Call of the Hawk

In the early morning darkness Tsena let himself down from the wagon and stood on both legs. There was no pain. Doctor Smithers had removed the splint the day before and said to go easy on his leg for a few days until he, the doctor, could find a horse to take him home. Tsena said nothing about his plan.

He tried a step. It was hard to lift his heel so he had to push off with his toes instead. Quietly he raised the bar and opened the heavy doors to the street. One of the horses snorted and stomped a hoof. The sky was still black, glittering with stars.

He sat on the ground, slipped the medicine bag over his head, and emptied its contents onto the flap of his breechcloth. One by one he took the holy things in his hands—first the tuft of white fur, then the grass and the smooth stone. He looked up at the stars and sang the song Spirit Wolf had taught him.

> *"The white wolves come running,*
> *The white wolves come running.*
> *Behold them and listen,*
> *Behold them and speak."*

He paused and then said, "O Spirit Wolf, hear my song for I need your power today."

He waited, but there was no answer. Was it because there was no moon? Or because Spirit Wolf would not call to him in a place with walls—as old Napawat said about coyote?

At last he went back inside the stable and put on the shirt and trousers Will had loaned him. He tied his braids on top of his head and fitted a *tejano* hat over them.

Soon the door creaked open. "Ready?" asked Will.

"*Sí,* ready."

Together they saddled Sandy in the dark, and Will led him out. The two boys mounted and rode through the streets. Here and there a dog barked, but no one opened a door to see who might be passing.

They followed the river as it wound south toward the mission. The eastern sky was beginning to lighten so they stayed close to the giant cypress trees that grew along the bank. Near the mission, the river curved east, leaving a meadow between it and the wall—the meadow where the horses were put out to graze.

Tsena looked for a hiding place. When they came to some low hanging branches, he said, "Here *bueno.*"

They dismounted and sat down under the tree to wait for the horses. Tsena felt a sense of uneasiness settle over him as he looked across the meadow at the high stone wall. The soldiers must not see him, for he could not bear the thought of being closed inside those walls again.

The sun was two fingers above the horizon when the east gate opened and the horses came crowding to get out. They whinnied and frolicked and shook their manes. Tsena saw the familiar reddish coat, the flowing golden tail as Yuaneh rushed ahead of the others into the meadow.

"There, you see? The red one that flies like the wind."

"Mmmm," Will said, "*muy hermosa.*"

Two soldiers rode out to watch over the herd. As soon as the horses settled down to graze, they dismounted and sat under a liveoak that grew near the wall.

Tsena and Will watched silently. When the sun had risen halfway up the sky, one of the men lay back in the grass and covered his face with his hat. Soon the other did the same.

Tsena waited. The horses nibbled the grass, moving

now and then to find more, and the soldiers slept. It was time.

"*Ahora*," Tsena whispered.

Will nodded.

Tsena put his hands around his mouth and called, "*Haw, haw, haw.*"

Yuaneh raised her head and looked toward the river. Only she seemed to know that it was not a hawk that called. The soldiers did not move. And except for an occasional swish of a tail or the shaking of a mane, the other horses went on cropping grass.

"She knows you!" Will whispered.

Again Tsena called.

Yuaneh started toward the river, slowly at first, her ears pricked. Then she broke into a trot. At that moment one of the soldiers jumped up and began shouting. He ran for his horse. The other soldier awoke and the two of them started after Yuaneh. Sandy began backing away while Will struggled to hold him.

"*Adelante!* Go!" Tsena said, motioning him away.

The soldiers were halfway across the meadow when Yuaneh reached the river. Tsena's heart hammered. He caught hold of the mane with one hand, leaped on, and they splashed through the water. Behind him, the soldiers shouted. He leaned over Yuaneh's neck and clung with his legs. The mare scrambled up the other bank, and together they flew.

He knew Yuaneh was faster than their horses. But

where to go? He could not follow Will into town. Should he outrun the soldiers and double back after dark? Or keep going? He looked around. The soldiers were riding hard. One of them raised his long gun and fired.

Will glanced back, then leaned over his horse and galloped on. Tsena drew closer to him. All at once Sandy's head went down. Will pitched forward over his neck onto the ground, and lay there.

Without thinking Tsena pulled Yuaneh to a stop and dropped down beside his friend.

Will rolled over on his back, his eyes big, his mouth open, gasping for breath.

"Go!" he managed, sitting up quickly.

Tsena stood, but it was too late. The soldiers were upon them, around them, jumping from their horses, pointing their guns.

They were young—one fat, the other wiry with a thin mustache. Even with wolf medicine Tsena could not look into the eyes of their guns and be sure bullets would not kill him. Now he knew he had thrown away his freedom. He could be on the other side of Béxar, if only he had kept going.

Mustache barked words at them.

Slowly, a little shakily, Will stood. He wiped his hair from his forehead and spoke. Tsena caught only a few words. *Smithers . . . Fisher . . .*

Mustache looked closely at Tsena, and all at once recognition came over his face.

"Take off your hat," he demanded in Spanish.

Tsena swept off the hat, and his black braids dropped to his shoulders.

Mustache said something that made Will stiffen. With his fists clenched he spoke a few clipped words in reply. Then to Tsena he said, "They take you back to the mission. I say to tell Colonel Fisher that my father comes to talk with him." He mounted Sandy. *"Hasta luego."*

Tsena nodded, but his heart lay on the ground. He had seen the hate in Colonel Fisher's eyes. Will turned his horse about and galloped off toward Béxar.

Mustache thrust a rope at Tsena and pointed to Yuaneh. When he had looped it around the mare's neck they started back to the mission. The soldiers rode on either side while Tsena walked, leading Yuaneh.

Inside the mission the heavy gates creaked shut, and the bar thudded into place, shutting him in. From the other side of the *iglesia* he heard the cracking explosions of target practice.

"Adelante," Mustache barked. "To Colonel Fisher."

Yuaneh followed him through the narrow corral. Once she came up and nuzzled Tsena's neck as if to say, *Here I am.*

Some soldiers grooming horses nearby stopped and watched them pass. One called out something and they all laughed. Tsena kept his eyes straight ahead, trying to look proud even though he did not feel it.

After tying Yuaneh, he limped on toward Colonel Fisher's quarters, prodded by Mustache's gun. He looked toward the far corner of the square. Children were galloping about on their stick horses while the women watched. One of them—it was Grandmother Moko—pointed in his direction. He flushed with shame and turned away. He could not do anything right—could not escape, could not take his own horse. Had Spirit Wolf forgotten him?

At Colonel Fisher's door the guard listened to Mustache and then stepped inside. Tsena's heartbeat quickened. If only Captain Redd were here.

When the guard reappeared he spoke to Mustache. Tsena did not understand the words, but Mustache looked pleased.

He shoved Tsena with his gun. "*Adelante,*" he shouted and jerked his head toward the far corner.

As Tsena hobbled along, his mind raced. *What has the colonel ordered? Are they going to shoot me? Will my wolf medicine protect me?*

The women and children stood and watched them. Moko struggled up and walked to Tsena's old door.

"Go away—move," Mustache told her. He opened the door, pushed Tsena inside, and slammed it shut.

"What you do with him?" Moko demanded in Spanish.

"I say go away, squaw!"

Through the cracks in the door Tsena could see that Mustache was standing guard. He heard the women

151

talking as they moved away, and once again the children mounted their stick horses.

Tsena sat down and opened his medicine bag. Taking out the tuft of fur, he lifted his face and quietly sang his song. Then he whispered, "O Spirit Wolf, send me a sign that my medicine is strong."

He put the fur back in the bag, let his head rest against the wall, and closed his eyes. There was nothing to do now but wait.

After a while he heard footsteps and someone talking to Mustache. Then Mustache flung the door open. "Colonel Fisher says you come *ahora*."

Tsena stepped outside. The women had gathered around, and Grandmother Moko began to sing. The others joined in as if he were going on the warpath. Their singing lifted him up, carried him toward the colonel's door. Then his heart leaped, for there, tied in front of the door, were Sandy and the doctor's black mare.

As Mustache pushed Tsena through the door, Will and the doctor turned. Will nodded slightly. Colonel Fisher sat behind the heavy table, the pupils in his pale blue eyes boring into Tsena.

"So, you try to escape," he began.

Tsena said nothing.

"I know what you Comanches do to captives who try to escape." He leaned forward. "You burn them . . . butcher them. Women and children. *Verdad?*"

Tsena said nothing.

"But we *tejanos* are different. We are not savages. We do not kill women and children."

Tsena felt hot anger rising inside him. He felt it flashing in his eyes. *No*, he wanted to shout, *you only kill chiefs in a peace council!*

The colonel stood abruptly. "I see the hate in your eyes, young savage. If the doctor was not my friend . . ." He breathed in sharply and looked away for a moment, then back at Tsena.

"But I cannot forget the favor he did for me. He wants me to let all the prisoners go—even you. So I am doing it for him." He pointed to the door. "Now get out of my sight and take your savage horse—before I change my mind."

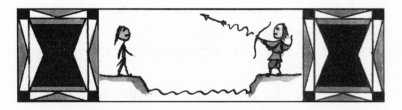

Shakespeare's Arrow

Twisting his fingers in Yuaneh's mane, Tsena pulled himself astride. The gate swung open, and he rode out between Will and the doctor. The sun was halfway down the sky, and the riders cast long shadows across the gentle slope as they descended into Béxar. For a time no one spoke.

The doctor is angry, thought Tsena. Still, his joy could not be contained. He was riding Yuaneh, he was free, and now he could go home. That sweet thought loosened the words he was holding back. Without turning he said, "I thank you for coming, Doctor."

Doctor Smithers did not reply at once. Then, smoothing his mustache, he said, "You and Will are very foolish. You make much worry for me—both of you."

The last three words echoed in Tsena's mind. This white man worried about him as if he were his own son.

He looked at the doctor then. "I have sorrow, Doctor. I think only of Yuaneh." He leaned forward and stroked the horse's neck. "You forgive?"

The doctor smiled. "I guess all is well that ends well, as Shakespeare says."

Will's face broke into a broad grin, and Tsena felt himself smiling too, though he was puzzled. "Shake . . . how do you say?" he began.

"Shake–speare," Doctor Smithers pronounced, his eyes glinting with amusement.

"*Will* Shakespeare," added Will. "I have his name."

"Will Shakespeare—he is a wise man?"

"*Sí*," said the doctor. "He lived nearly three hundred years ago, on the other side of the ocean."

Tsena turned to Will. "You read his signs?"

"*Sí*, I show to you."

At the stable door they reined in, and Doctor Smithers said, "If you like we have dinner for *adios* tomorrow."

Tsena nodded. "*Gracias, Señor* Doctor. I like very much."

That night after supper, as Tsena sat under the

green berry tree, Will came out with a lantern in one hand and a book in the other. It was a thick book covered in red leather with gold-edged pages.

"Here is Shakespeare. I read some of his words." He set the lantern on the bench and sat down beside Tsena. "You do not understand, but I read anyway." He took out his spectacles, curled the gold handles around his ears, and turned some pages. Signs and more signs and pictures too—a man with a donkey's head and men in metal clothes riding horses.

Then Will began to read. The words rolled from his tongue like words of a song.

When he stopped, Tsena asked, "What means the words?"

"They are the last words of *All Is Well that Ends Well*. They mean something like . . . if the past is bitter, more welcome is the sweet."

Tsena pondered them. *If the past is bitter, more welcome is the sweet.* Yes, Shakespeare spoke the truth. It would not be as sweet to have Yuaneh now if he had never lost her. Nor would it be as sweet to return home if he had not been a prisoner.

It seemed to Tsena that Shakespeare had shot an arrow across three hundred winters and pierced a hole in his world, letting in light. One day he would learn more of white man's signs so he could read three-hundred-year-old words. One day. But now was the time for going home.

At breakfast the next morning in the patio, Will said, "I have no lessons. What do you want to do on your last day here?"

Tsena was pleased because there was something he had been thinking of ever since the doctor invited him to the dinner for *adios*.

"I want to write signs on paper for a gift," he said. "Can you help me?"

Will grinned. "Of course. Come, let's go to my room."

Like the rest of the *casa*, his room had white walls and a dark polished floor. He shared it with *Señor* Peck, who "by fortune is still at breakfast," said Will.

By fortune, yes, thought Tsena. The man did not seem to consider him to be human, much less a *true* human.

Will put on his spectacles and sat down at a table. From a wooden box he took out his writing materials—a quill, a sheet of paper, bottle of ink, and a small tin can with holes in the top. Folding the paper back and forth several times, he carefully tore it in two parts.

"Now, what do you want to write?"

Tsena took a deep breath and spoke slowly, spacing each word. "I—thank—you—for—your—kindness. I—never—forget."

Will nodded. He dipped the quill in ink and wrote many signs. Then he handed it to Tsena. "Now, practice once."

Tsena sat down and swept his braids back over his

shoulders. Gripping the quill between his thumb and first two fingers, he dipped the point in the bottle. As he touched it to paper, ink ran down and made a black blob.

"*Och*, no good." This was not going to be as easy as writing with a stick in the dirt.

"Do not worry—I did many times." Will showed him how to wipe the point before taking it from the ink bottle.

The pen scratched as Tsena carefully copied what Will had written, often stopping in the middle of a sign to take another look. His lines thickened when he stopped, wobbled and leaned, but Will said it was good enough to read. After he had practiced all the signs, he wrote them on the other sheet of paper with only one small blob.

Will sprinkled a light coating of sand over it "to make dry," he explained. Then he poured the sand back into the shaker.

"*Excelente*," he said, stretching his neck and looking down at Tsena like *Señor* Peck. Tsena laughed.

Footsteps sounded in the hall, and suddenly *Señor* Peck himself stood in the doorway, his lips pursed. Tsena stood up beside the chair.

The teacher remained there for a moment taking in the scene. Then he spoke to Will in white man's words.

Will replied, snatched Tsena's letter from the desk, and motioned him to follow.

"What he says?" Tsena asked as soon as they were out in the patio.

"*Nada*," Will replied, scowling. "Not important."

"I know," Tsena persisted, "he says I cannot come in your room, *verdad?*"

"Something like that," Will answered, heading into the *casa* for cooking.

Carmencita looked around from washing dishes.

"*Por favor*, Carmencita, may we use the table?" Will asked.

"*Sí, claro.*" She dried her hands and came over to look at what they were doing.

Quickly, before she could see it, Will folded the letter in three parts. "No, Carmencita, you have to wait until tonight."

She nodded, patting Tsena on the shoulder. "Smart boy. I knew it all the time."

"Tell *Señor* Peck," Will said.

She went back to her dish pan. "Ahh, he sees only the end of his nose."

Tsena and Will laughed, and the strain was broken. Carmencita took the dishes out, carried the pan to the door, and emptied the dirty water on a vine that grew just outside. It seemed to Tsena that *Señor* Peck's words—whatever they meant—went with it.

Will brought a candle and sealed the letter with a drop of wax. He pushed it toward Tsena, handing him a knife. "Now, make a *T* here."

Tsena pressed two lines into the soft wax in the shape of a *T*, and it was done.

That afternoon he bathed in the small *casa* beside the garden. Then he put on his breechcloth and his leggings that Carmencita had mended. And last of all a blue shirt she made for him. He ran his hands over the smooth, shiny cloth called *seda*. In such a shirt he could feel proud at the party—even with *Señor* Peck. Looking in the mirror he combed his hair and braided it with strips of blue *seda* left over from the shirt.

After darkness fell they gathered around the table in the Long Room and sat down in chairs. Candlelight reflected in the glasses that stood like flowers on slender stalks. Tsena looked down at the silver utensils on either side of his plate. What was he to do with all of them? And what if he spilled something on the snowy white cloth? It seemed that everyone was watching him to see what mistake he would make.

For a moment he wanted to bolt from the room, but instead he watched Will, who sat beside him, and Agatha, who sat across the table. She smiled and bowed her head as did Will and everyone else. Tsena bowed his head. This was white man's way of speaking to their god—looking down, not up in the *Nemena* way. Doctor Smithers said a prayer in Spanish, thanking their god for food. He ended his prayer by saying,

> *"Bless this boy, Tsena,*
> *On his way home,*
> *And give peace*
> *To all men on earth. Amen."*

The words struck deep in Tsena's heart and kindled a warm feeling for the people gathered around this table. Except for *Señor* Peck.

After the prayer Will took the small, folded cloth from beside his plate, shook it out, and placed it on his lap. Tsena did the same. He watched Will pick up his knife and fork, spear a piece of roast beef with his fork and slice off a small bite with his knife. Then he lay the knife across his plate, took the fork in his right hand, and put the bite in his mouth. Tsena tried to do the same, but too late he realized he had not changed the fork to his right hand. He looked around the table, but no one seemed to notice. He took a deep breath and felt some of the tension melt away.

Señor Peck talked with the doctor at one end of the table. *Señora* Smithers, at the other end, turned to Tsena.

"You are happy to go home, *verdad*?"

Never had he been this near her. Even though she was a plump woman, she had fine, delicate features and the palest skin he had ever seen.

"*Sí, verdad*, but I miss very much the people of this *casa*."

Agatha's eyes brightened. "If you stay, Tsena, I can teach you to read more." She looked at *Señor* Peck beside her.

Tsena smiled. "I like but . . . I am son of a chief. I have to return to the *Nemena*."

When Carmencita brought *piloncillos* and coffee, Will reached in his pocket and handed Tsena a small metal box. "I give this to you."

Tsena held it in his palm. He had not expected a gift. As he looked around the table at the pale faces glowing in the candlelight, all watching him, not even the sight of *Señor* Peck could cast a shadow.

"Open it, Tsena," said Agatha impatiently.

Inside, a piece of flint and a curved steel lay on shreds of cloth. It was a tinder box. He had seen such a box before.

"You know how to use it?" Will asked.

Tsena picked up the flint and steel and pretended to strike them together over the cloth tinder. "Like so, *verdad?*"

Will nodded.

"*Gracias*, I like very much." His words scarcely seemed enough. Then remembering his own gift, he pulled the letter from his shirt pocket and handed it to the doctor. "I write this for everyone."

Doctor Smithers opened the seal with his slender fingers and read aloud, "I thank you for your kindness. I never forget." His mustache curled up. "*De nada*, my boy."

Tsena glanced at *Señor* Peck. For one unguarded moment the teacher was studying him with interest.

Carmencita, who had been holding the tray all this time, set it on the table and to Tsena's surprise wrapped her arms around his shoulders. "You are not only a smart boy but a good one too," she said.

Then Agatha took a folded paper from her lap. "I made a story for you." She unfolded it and read aloud in white man's words, emphasizing the ones she had taught him.

> "One day a *Comanche* boy came
> to our *house*. His name is *Tsena*.
> I was very frightened. Then he
> taught me the game of *hands*. *I*
> taught him to *read* and *write*
> some words. Now we are *friends*.
> Goodbye *Tsena*. Your *friend Agatha*."

The family clapped their hands, and Agatha handed it across the table to Tsena. He looked at the many signs, but could understand only a few. Will leaned closer and, pointing at the signs, translated them into Spanish.

When Tsena understood, he looked at Agatha. "*Gracias*. I keep for all my days." He folded the paper until it was small enough to fit in his medicine bag.

"The *Nemena* say the heart does not have a tongue. Now my heart is full, but I have no words."

"You Are Different"

Ridge after ridge of blue hills stretched before him in the distance as Tsena started home. But his thoughts reached back to the people he had left behind that morning. Carmencita had tears in her eyes, and Agatha's golden curls bobbed as she ran alongside him for a way. The doctor and his *señora* waved until he was out of sight, while Will stood with one arm raised, in the *Nemena* way. That gesture burned itself into Tsena's mind, and he knew that he would never forget it.

After a time he turned his thoughts to the long journey ahead. He and Yuaneh would cross the Guadalupe River, then the Pedernales, the Llano, and come finally to Lone Hill.

It was the Moon of Blooming Meadows. Tsena took a deep breath, filling his lungs with the smell of blue flowers that covered the rolling land. How good it felt to be outside of walls and going home.

They rode up into steep, rocky hills that looked more and more like home. Toward nightfall, wind began to sough in the liveoak branches. As Yuaneh picked her way up a crumbling slope, Tsena leaned forward and patted her neck.

"It cannot be far to the Guadalupe, my little mare." She swiveled her ears to hear his words. "Then you can rest and make your belly full until the moon rises."

Sometime after dark Tsena heard rushing water and saw an even darker line of trees ahead—the Guadalupe. At the river's edge he dismounted, and he and Yuaneh drank side by side. Then he ate a stick of jerky that Carmencita had packed. After unrolling a blanket, he lay back, looking at the Evening Star in the west.

Perhaps Anawakeo was looking at the Evening Star too. He had not thought of her for many sleeps but now he longed to see her again. He closed his eyes and remembered how she looked at him from the corners of her dark eyes. How she tilted her head to one side whenever she smiled at him. At last, the sound of water purling over rocks lulled him to sleep.

When he awoke, the bulging moon had risen halfway up the sky and its reflection played in the river. Yuaneh stood nearby, and as soon as Tsena sat up she came to him.

"Ready, my little mare?"

She whinnied and tossed her head, which meant *yes*.

Through the moonlit night they rode, heading west of the Star That Does Not Walk Around. Slowly the sky began to glow in the east—first pale orange, then fiery red. Tsena dismounted to await the sun.

When the first rays flashed over the distant hills, he raised his arms. "Let your power enter my body, Father Sun." He stood motionless with his eyes closed, letting the warmth soak into his skin until Yuaneh blew through her nose.

Then he mounted and rode on. While the sun climbed the sky, they climbed hill after hill, splashed through creeks, and crossed the Pedernales River.

The sun reached its zenith and started down. By the time they came to the broad, shallow Llano it was only two fingers above the horizon, turning the water pale red like the sky. Tsena urged Yuaneh on. As they came out of the valley he saw Lone Hill in the distance. Many smoke plumes were rising to the west.

"Yuaneh, we are home!"

The mare already knew, for she began to trot without any urging. At the edge of a meadow Tsena stopped in a clump of liveoaks, scarcely a bowshot away from the village. No one had seen him. Not even the dogs had heard him or caught his scent. Children played amongst the lodges and women gathered firewood along the creek on the far side of the village. There was his mother stooping to pick up a branch.

Tsena nudged Yuaneh with his heels, out into the meadow. He raised his arm, and called, "It is Tsena! I have returned!"

The dogs began barking, women turned to look, men came out of the lodges, and children stopped their play.

"Tsena!" called Topay. The firewood fell from her arms, and she ran to Grandfather Ahsenap's lodge. Together they came out to meet him, leading the whole village. Ahsenap moved slowly on his old bowed legs while Topay sang her joy in a high, wavering voice. The other women joined in, and the children ran ahead. Chawakeh stopped a short distance away, watching him with eyes that seemed darker than before.

Tsena limped to Grandfather Ahsenap and they embraced.

Stepping back, Ahsenap looked him over with his one good eye. "Why do you walk like an old one, Grandson?"

Tsena laughed. "An old one who grows younger every day, Grandfather." He told how he had jumped from the mission wall and broken his ankle.

Ahsenap nodded, studying him. In a moment he went on. "You are different in a more important way."

"Yes, Grandfather. Spirit Wolf came to me in a vision and gave me his medicine. And a name. I am to be called Tsena Naku, He Who Hears the Wolf."

Ahsenap put his hand on Tsena's shoulder. "Tsena Naku," he repeated. "It is a name that carries power, Grandson. And wolf medicine gives you wise ferocity."

"Yes, Grandfather." Then pulling the gun barrel from his belt, Tsena said, "This is from the *tejano* who shot Father. He will not need it again."

Ahsenap took the barrel and studied it. He looked up at Tsena, his eye shining. "Tonight you will tell the whole village your story, Grandson. I will ask Toyama to send out a crier."

"And tomorrow I shall make your man-lodge," said Topay.

After Ahsenap left to speak with Toyama, everyone crowded around, greeting him, asking him questions. No one spoke the name of his father, for that would show lack of respect.

Tsena put his hands on Kianceta's shoulders. "I am happy to see you again, Ceta."

The younger boy grinned. "And I you, Tsena Naku."

"How is old Pahtooeh?" Tsena asked.

"Still full of sand."

They both laughed.

Later, when he had bathed in the creek, Tsena tethered Yuaneh beside his mother's lodge. She stepped out holding a pair of leggings and beaded moccasins and a blue breechcloth. "Here, my son, I made these while waiting for you to return. Wear them to the feast tonight."

"I will, Mother, thank you. Now I can be proud to stand up and tell my story." He took the new clothes from her and looked down at them for a moment without speaking.

"Is something wrong, my son?"

"You must leave the circle before I tell my story—it will be too painful for you to remember."

She nodded.

"And something else. I was just wondering if Toyama is a good . . . a good peace chief?"

She shook her head sadly. "No, he is weak. The people listen to Isimanica now."

"But surely he is not chief of the Twelve Bands, is he?"

"No, thank the spirits. It is Pochana Quoheep."

Tsena nodded, relieved. He remembered the young pock-faced chief from the tribal council so long ago.

"And . . . what about the old chief's granddaughter? Did she return?" He felt his cheeks grow hot.

A smile flickered at the corners of her mouth. "Yes, my son. A messenger brought the news and asked after you."

Tsena's heart gave a little leap of joy. It was no longer a question of whether he would see her again— but when.

That night a fire was built in the center of the village. Tsena, his grandfather, and Toyama sat to one side of Isimanica with Tsena's half-brother, Kiyou, on the other. Kiyou said little, but Tsena had seen him looking at the gun barrel in his belt. It seemed to silence his bad tongue, for tonight at least.

When the music and dancing stopped, Ahsenap rose to speak. In his gritty voice he said, "Tonight we celebrate the return of my grandson. He has had a vision, and henceforth he shall be known as Tsena Naku."

Tsena stood. "Thank you, Grandfather." As he walked to the center of the circle, his heart began to gallop. Everyone's eyes were on him. They all waited for his story. He hesitated, watching the firelight flicker on the surrounding lodges, and then he began.

"Hear me, for I tell the story of the massacre in the council lodge and my revenge." His breath was short as if he had been running across the meadow. But when he began to see the images of his story, he forgot his fright.

"Father Sun stood at the zenith as our chiefs and theirs sat facing one another in the council lodge." Tsena sat down, his back to the fire. He told of the exchange of words between the chief of the Twelve Bands and the *tejano* chief. Then he stood, telling how the soldiers surrounded them and the *tejano* chief said they were prisoners. How the chiefs rushed for the door and killed the soldier who blocked it. And how his father had escaped and they ran for the creek.

"Then around the corner came a mounted *tejano*. His gun spit fire at my father." Tsena was trembling and felt his knees might fold under him. He glanced at Kiyou,

170

who was absorbed by the story, and that gave him new strength.

"I raised my bow, pulled the arrow to the head, and let it fly. It pierced his shoulder. He rode at me and kicked the bow from my hand and pointed his gun at me."

Tsena pulled the barrel from his belt and held it up with both hands. "I grabbed the barrel and it came off. The gun exploded in his face."

Then, walking around the circle, holding the barrel on high, Tsena said, "The *tejano* who fired this gun will never kill again. My father is revenged. That is all."

The musicians pounded their drums. People yelled, "*Yip, yip, yip!*" They stamped their feet and clapped as he sat down.

Isimanica stood, his huge body gleaming with bear grease. He held up his arm for silence. "It is a brave deed which you have done, Tsena Naku. Your father has been revenged. But the time will come for us to go with our brothers and revenge the other chiefs. I have spoken."

It was as old Napawat predicted. What was Tsena to do? What about his solemn promise to Father? What about the good *tejanos*? But he knew, deep in that dark place where one hides what he does not want to think on, that he had no choice.

Later that night Topay spread his sleeping robes outside.

"When the time comes," she said, "you must join the

171

war party and follow Isimanica, in spite of your promise. I want white women to suffer as I have."

Tsena said nothing. He could not tell her about the white boy who had rescued him, or the white doctor who had cared for him, or the white girl who wanted to teach him to read. More and more he felt like Lone Hill.

Long after the whole village slept, Tsena lay awake. Tree frogs were trilling to each other back and forth across the creek when a rustling sound nearby startled him. He sat up quickly. It was Ahsenap.

He came and sat down beside Tsena, pulling his robe close around him, for the night air had grown chill.

"You told your story with much skill, Grandson."

"Thank you, Grandfather."

The old man's white hair shone in the moonlight as he gazed into the night.

"I sense there is more," he said at last.

"You see inside my heart, Grandfather."

He nodded.

"It is true," Tsena said. "I did not tell that a *tejano* family took me in—fed me and gave me a place to sleep while my leg healed." He opened his medicine bag and took out the folded letter.

"One of them, a small girl, wrote signs on this paper for me," he explained. "It says that she was frightened when I came to her house. But that I taught her to play the hand game, and she taught me how to read and write some signs. So we became friends."

Leaning toward the old man, he pointed out a word on the moonlit paper. "Look, Grandfather, this says *Tsena*. And here, this is white man's word for *friend*." His voice grew louder, more excited. He wanted to tell Grandfather the other words he knew and explain about Will Shakespeare.

The old man held up his hand. "Softly, Grandson, softly. Others may be listening."

Lowering his voice Tsena went on to tell the story he had not told around the fire. When he was finished, Ahsenap nodded thoughtfully.

"You have learned much, Grandson—even more than words."

"But the more I learn, Grandfather, the less I know. I promised Father to follow his dream of peace—even though my blood was on fire. And now that I have known the enemy and the fire has burned down, I must go on the warpath."

Grandfather rubbed his legs, which sometimes grew numb when he sat too long. "Our people have revenge in their hearts. I fear it will not be cooled without spilling *tejano* blood. So you too must go." He held up his hand. "But a time will come when we must make peace or be destroyed. That will be your time."

The Word Comes

It was during the Moon when Buffalo Bellow that a messenger came from Pochana Quoheep saying he had received a sign. He had seen an eagle swoop down and seize a small white rabbit. "Thus will we swoop down on the *tejanos* and take revenge," he said. "When this moon is old let us gather where the Llano flows into the Colorado."

The time that Tsena dreaded had come.

Isimanica called for a council at once, and Tsena went with his grandfather. Even with the lodge cover rolled up, there was no breeze to stir the sweltering air. The councilors fanned themselves and waited as the sacred pipe was passed.

174

In turn, Ahsenap took the pipe in his old veined hand and smoked. Then he looked over his shoulder and offered it to Tsena for the first time. It was his way of saying, *You are a warrior now. You can keep your promise later.*

Tsena nodded and took the pipe in his hands. It seemed to quiver with life. He brought the mouthpiece to his lips and drew the breath of the Great Spirit down into his body. Its power made his head swirl.

When the pipe was returned to Isimanica, he hefted himself up and stood with his arms folded over his chest. A slow smile spread across his face.

"Good news comes to us this day," he said. "Soon the *Nemena* will assemble in a great war party. It is time for us to make our weapons ready and gather provisions. Therefore I call for our summer hunt to begin two sleeps hence. What say you, Toyama?"

The peace chief arose. He had a kindly face like Quasia's, but Tsena could see that his eyes lacked the passion of his father's eyes. And without passion whatever he said would make no difference. Isimanica had it—and everyone listened.

"I must disagree with you," Toyama began in a droning voice. "It is not good news. We have no reason to go on the warpath. Our chief has been revenged by his son." He paused.

Tsena felt himself flush as several chiefs turned to look at him. Even though he agreed, he kept his face still.

175

"And what about the captives our people killed?" Toyama went on. "Do you not call that revenge?"

Isimanica stood again and dismissed Toyama's words—and seemingly Tsena—with a wave of his hand. "A few miserable captives are no revenge for killing twelve chiefs. I say, let us paint our faces with black and rid the earth of *tejanos*. That is all."

Ahsenap motioned that he wanted to stand. Tsena helped him to his feet and stood behind him. Whatever his grandfather's words might be, they would be his words too.

"I say," Ahsenap began, the words grating in his throat, "we must join with the other bands to take vengeance. But let us be the voice of moderation among them. Let us be satisfied with twelve scalps for twelve chiefs. Thus would we leave the lodge door open for peace."

Isimanica leaped up. Glaring at Ahsenap, he spaced his words. "Twelve scalps do not equal twelve chiefs." He spread his feet, put his hands on his hips, and looked around the circle. "No, the debt of the *tejanos* will not be paid until their blood soaks the land."

"It will be our blood too," Ahsenap said.

"If we listened to old men in matters of war, Grandfather, we would soon be pushed north onto the hunting grounds of the Cheyenne." He turned and addressed the other councilors. "Pochana Quoheep has good medicine. The white rabbit was destroyed. So will it be with the *tejanos* and their seed. I have spoken."

Ahsenap said no more. He sat nodding his head slightly. Tsena wondered if it would be his blood that Grandfather meant.

Other councilors arose and spoke, agreeing with the war chief. The *tejanos*, they decided, must pay a great price for the massacre.

"You make my heart glad," said Isimanica. "Now let us prepare."

A plan began to form in Tsena's mind. He would go to Pochana Quoheep himself and tell him of Grandfather's concern. Being the son of one of the slain chiefs, Tsena certainly would be heard. But would he make a difference?

Two sleeps later at first light, Isimanica raised his bow, and the assembled hunting party began to move. Kiyou rode at his uncle's side in the lead, while Tsena and Kianceta followed. This was Kianceta's first time to run buffalo, and Tsena knew he was afraid because he was so quiet.

Tsena leaned close to him and whispered, "Are you afraid?"

Kianceta laughed a sudden kind of laugh that has little to do with anything being funny. "Yes," he admitted, "I would not tell anyone else, but I am."

"So am I," said Tsena. "So is everyone, especially before his first run—even Kiyou."

"Truly?"

Tsena nodded. "Last year before I killed my first buffalo, I had to make my heart like a fist and tell myself I was not afraid."

"That is what I keep telling myself," said Kianceta, "but the trouble is, I do not believe me."

Tsena laughed. "Then believe me, Ceta." He made a fist over his heart. "You are not afraid. Your heart is a fist."

"If you say so, Chief Tsena Naku!"

They both laughed.

At the sound of their laughter, Kiyou looked around. Then he turned and rode back to them, wheeling his horse about sharply. Tsena felt the laughter die in his throat.

"They say you love *tejanos*, Grandfather." Kiyou spat on the ground.

Grandfather Ahsenap was right, thought Tsena. Someone had overheard him talking that first night. He knew he should ignore Kiyou, but he could not. "You make my heart tired, Coyote Mouth."

"Insults don't hide the truth, Grandfather. Do you or not?"

Tsena did not want to bring out his feelings and lay them bare for Kiyou. He would not tell him about Will and the doctor and Shakespeare. Yet he had to answer.

He lifted his chin and said, "What if I did make friends of some? Even the old chief of the Twelve Bands had a white friend."

But Kiyou did not seem to hear the last part. He threw back his head. "*Och*, I was wrong. You are no grandfather. Only a woman would make friends with the enemy." He gave his horse the quirt and rode back to the head of the procession.

He who controls himself . . . He who controls himself . . . Grandfather's words throbbed in his head.

"Do not bother yourself over him, Tsena," Kianceta murmured. "He is just jealous of your barrel coup."

Still, Tsena *was* bothered by him and, later, by his uncle as well. Several times during the long, hot ride Isimanica looked over his shoulder toward the rear of the procession where the women were. Once he turned his horse and rode back there. Tsena watched him go by, his silver breastplate jiggling. To Tsena's horror, he stopped when he reached Topay, wheeled his horse about, and rode alongside her.

How dare he, thought Tsena, *when she is still in mourning.* Fury blazed up inside him. It seemed the war chief wanted to dishonor Quasia's memory by making his wife love him. Tsena turned away, and again Grandfather's words came to him. He repeated them over and over until the fury died down.

That evening Isimanica signaled a halt at the edge of a plateau. The valley below was black with grazing buffalo, like a dark lake rippled by the wind. He tossed a feather in the air, and it floated back over their heads.

"We camp here," he said, "where the old bulls will not catch our scent."

The sun was sinking rapidly as the women made camp. Topay and Chawakeh set up two small tents, but

179

no one built a fire that night. Chawakeh was almost too tired to eat, and only by coaxing did Topay get her to take a few bites of pemmican. She had spent most of the day running about with other children as the procession moved along. Now she crawled in the tent and curled up on her robe.

Topay was tying up the parfleche that held their food. Tsena could not go to bed without saying what was on his mind.

"It does not please me that Isimanica gives you attention, Mother."

She covered her mouth and looked at him.

Was she hiding a smile under her hand? he wondered. "Surely you do not enjoy his attention."

"No, my son, surely not. I am smiling because you make me happy." Then she grew serious. "Never think that I could forget your father or become Isimanica's wife. Neither do I wish to insult him—for he can help us."

"We do not need his help, Mother. I am a man now. Your lodge will never lack for meat."

"I know that, but if you are to be chief one day, you must not make enemies."

"If you encourage him," Tsena said, "he will be angrier than ever when he discovers that you will not be his wife."

"No." She shook her head. "He is a fickle man and impatient too. He will grow weary of waiting through my period of mourning and find a younger woman."

Shrugging, she added, "Or get himself killed on the warpath."

Yes, maybe so, thought Tsena. A sudden uneasiness came over him as he thought of that warpath—his first, one which he did not want to go on, but must.

By dawn the next morning the herd of buffalo had moved closer to the mouth of the valley where it opened onto a great plain. Warriors mounted their horses and gathered around Isimanica. He surveyed them with his black slit eyes that looked more evil than ever to Tsena.

"I remind you," said the chief, "no one is to charge until I give the signal." His eyes slid to rest on Kiyou, then Tsena and the other young hunters. "You will ride along the sides of the herd and keep it from spreading out." Then he opened his arms to the earth and sky. "May the spirits favor us."

Slowly and quietly they descended into the valley and formed a great crescent—Isimanica in the center, Tsena and Kiyou on the right horn. Kianceta rode nearby with his father. The buffalo grazed, peacefully unaware.

Tsena's heart began to pound. He remembered how his father had ridden beside him, pressing him closer to the buffalo. Now he was alone, and he must make a kill. Mother had no one else. The very thought emboldened him.

He glanced over at Kianceta, who looked back at him. Tsena put his fist over his heart. Kianceta nodded and made the same sign.

An old bull at the edge of the herd raised his huge

head and sniffed the air. Suddenly, he struck the ground with his hoof—once, twice, three times. The herd began to run.

Isimanica raised his bow, and the warriors sprang into a gallop. Tsena raced along the right side of the herd. It was like racing thunder across the sky. Here and there a buffalo fell, while the others ran on, their heads down, tails arched, horns clacking together—a sound that still struck terror in Tsena's heart.

Up ahead a bull broke away. Tsena nudged Yuaneh with his knee, and the mare turned toward him as though she understood this one was theirs. Tsena nocked an arrow and aimed at the soft spot behind the ribs. His muscles trembled as he struggled to hold a steady aim. He let the string go, but the arrow flew high, hitting the hump.

At the twang of the string Yuaneh veered off as Tsena had trained her to do, and the bull ran on. Tsena pulled another arrow and nudged Yuaneh back toward the buffalo, closer this time. He could feel the heat of the great humped body. He drew the string back and let the arrow fly. It plunged deep into the bull's side. Again the mare veered off, but the buffalo turned sharply, lowered his head, and charged at Yuaneh. Blood bubbled from his nose.

Suddenly, Kiyou appeared from behind, shot an arrow into the bull's other side, and galloped on. The animal staggered, then his front legs buckled only a few strides away. Tsena rode on, his heart pounding against his chest as if it wanted to get out. He could hear the buffalo bellowing his death song. *Had Kiyou meant to save Yuaneh from being gored?* he wondered.

The herd was scattering across the plain that was now littered with fallen buffalo. Isimanica signaled an end to the hunt.

Tsena turned Yuaneh about and came back to his kill. He dismounted and raised his arms to give thanks.

> "O, sacred buffalo,
> You gave your life to me.
> For that I give you thanks,
> And set your spirit free."

Kiyou rode up then, jumped off his horse, and stood beside the buffalo. With his hands on his hips he said, "This is my kill."

Tsena threw his head back. How could he have imagined anything noble from Kiyou? "No, it is my kill. My arrow brought blood to his mouth."

"All I know is that my arrow stopped him in his tracks—or else your horse would be meat for the warpath."

It was true. Whether Kiyou intended or not, he had saved Yuaneh's life—perhaps even Tsena's. And Tsena did not know what to make of that truth. He did know that he could not force himself to thank Kiyou. The words simply could not get through his throat.

He looked away, across the valley where warriors

were returning to skin their buffalo. Even Kianceta had killed a calf and stood over it with his arms raised. Tsena felt himself smiling at the sight. At least his friend had done well.

"Here comes my uncle," said Kiyou and grinned. "He will decide which of us made the kill."

Tsena knew it was Isimanica's duty as the hunt chief to settle any disputes. Ordinarily there would be little hope of a fair decision between himself and Kiyou. But now that the chief seemed to be courting Topay, perhaps . . .

Isimanica stopped, looking at the two boys and the buffalo between them. He seemed to be trying to decide what to do.

"Uncle," Kiyou said, "it was my arrow here that brought the buffalo down after Tsena's pricked him into rage."

"No," Tsena protested, "my shot—here," he pointed to his arrow, "pierced his heart and made blood foam from his nose."

Isimanica glanced over his shoulder. "Here come the women," he said. "I would not have them see us quarreling. Therefore, this kill shall be divided equally between you."

That night, after hunting stories were told around the fire, Tsena lay in his tent thinking back on the strange day. Kiyou had saved Yuaneh from being gored, whether he intended to or not. And for that Tsena owed him something.

21

Down the Warpath

The Moon of Long Days grew old, and it was time to go. Twice Tsena had gone up to Lone Hill and sung his song to Spirit Wolf, but he had not received a sign. Was his guardian spirit offended by this warpath? Did he wish Tsena to keep his promise to Quasia? It was worrisome, but Tsena said nothing to anyone, not even to his grandfather.

On the night of leaving, a fire was built in the center of the village. In his man-lodge, Tsena held a mirror in one hand, dipped his finger into the paint, and drew a black stripe across his cheek. The color of death, he thought, but he did not know whose. Already the drummers were beginning to beat their drums. He drew one

185

last stripe from his hairline down the ridge of his nose. Then he put away his powders and ducked out of the opening.

Low clouds held the heat of day upon the village, and the air throbbed with drumbeats. Light from the fire shone on the faces of women and children and old men seated around it, as they watched the warriors dance. Grandfather Ahsenap, his mouth set, watched with his one sharp eye.

Tsena stepped into the circle alongside Kianceta. The beat of the drums took hold of his body, and he began to stomp around the fire, toe-heel, toe-heel. Kiyou held up his battle axe as he danced. He looked at Tsena with a sneer, but it did not matter. Nothing mattered but the throbbing rhythm. It drove all thoughts from his head.

"*Aieeeee,*" someone cried, and Tsena threw back his head and heard himself yell, "*Aieeeee, aieeeee.*" Sweat ran down his face, his body, his arms.

At last Isimanica stopped and held up his arms. The drumming ceased, the warriors stopped dancing and sat in place. When all was still, the chief folded his arms and spoke. "Tonight we go forth to revenge our chiefs. I ask you, warriors of the *Nemena*, to show your courage so that your families can take pride in your deeds. May our *puha* be strong. That is all."

Warriors leaped up, yipping, and Tsena leaped with them. Drummers pounded their drums for one last dance around the fire. Then, one by one, they all stomped out of the circle to their horses.

Tsena found his family waiting at his lodge where Yuaneh and the trail horse were staked. Silently he shouldered his bowcase, slipped Grandfather's medicine shield over his arm, and mounted Yuaneh. Thoughts began to seep back into his head. He was leaving on his first warpath, and that was a more frightening thought than going on his first buffalo run.

"Is he coming back or is he going to be killed like Father?" Chawakeh asked.

Topay sucked in a breath and pulled the little girl to her. Only children could ask such a question, even though everyone was thinking it—including Tsena. For a moment her question hung in the air.

Tsena could not answer his sister directly now that he was a man. "Tell her not to worry. I have wolf medicine and Grandfather's shield." He held it up. "They will protect me," he said, though he was not sure.

Ahsenap checked the loop he had braided into Yuaneh's mane. Then he put his hand on Tsena's leg as if he were still a child. "Yes, Grandson, but you must believe it."

Tsena looked down at the old man's face. Firelight made his wrinkles look even deeper. It seemed that Grandfather had always been able to see into his mind. *Now he sees my doubts*, thought Tsena. Suddenly, he wondered if his grandfather would be here when he returned. He reached out and put his hand on Ahsenap's shoulder. "Yes, Grandfather, I will believe it if you will wait for me."

"I will wait for you, Grandson."

It was time to leave. Following Isimanica, the mounted warriors began to move out of the village, leading trail horses. Yuaneh pulled on the rein, anxious to be off. Ahsenap handed Tsena the trail horse's rope and stepped back. Tsena raised his hand in a silent farewell to his family and gave Yuaneh a little nudge.

Away from the village they rode, into the darkness. In front of him was Kiyou and behind rode Kianceta. No one talked as the horses picked their way across the rocky ground. This was to be a long warpath, all the way to the Great Water. The married warriors were bringing their wives, who rode at the rear of the procession, pulling travois loaded with all the comforts of their lodges.

They passed Lone Hill, looming in the night sky. In spite of all the people around him, Tsena felt as lonely as that hill . . . as he had many times in the past. No one except Grandfather knew that his heart was not in this war of revenge. And maybe Kiyou.

At the Llano they stopped to camp for the rest of the night. Tsena staked Yuaneh and the trail horse, a shaggy brown creature named Nooki. Then he lay down on his buffalo hide next to Kianceta, each in his own thoughts about what was to be.

Tsena closed his eyes. If only Spirit Wolf would call

to him or give him a sign. Gradually the gentle sounds of the river purling against the bank and the horses cropping the grass lulled him to sleep.

It seemed he had no sooner fallen asleep than the camp stirred awake. How different things seemed at dawn than in the dark of night. Today they would reach the Colorado, and he would talk to Pochana Quoheep. There was something comforting about that—some hope that this warpath would not mean death to everyone in its way.

After bathing in the river, Tsena and Kianceta opened their saddle bags. "My mother has packed enough for many sleeps," said Kianceta.

"Mine too." Tsena leaned closer and whispered, "We will get as fat as Isimanica."

"And our chests will jiggle like a woman's," Kianceta added.

Tsena laughed. "What would I do without your funny tongue, Ceta?"

"Or I without your laugh?"

"I guess we would worry about things that might happen," Tsena said.

Kianceta nodded.

As Tsena tied the riding pad on Nooki, Yuaneh raised her head and swiveled her ears.

"I am letting you rest today, my little mare, but you are still my favorite," Tsena said. "I am saving you for the time I need you most."

189

Yuaneh came closer and nuzzled him.

All that day the war party moved on toward the Colorado while the summer sun blazed down on them. Yuaneh trailed along behind. Once she trotted up and nipped the other horse. Nooki jumped forward, but Tsena just laughed and looked back at Yuaneh. "Shame on you, my beauty."

Along the way Tsena thought about the words he would speak to Pochana Quoheep. They must be carefully chosen. He would not use Ahsenap's idea of moderation. It sounded too much like defeat, and the chief would close his ears. No, he would talk of honor—an honorable revenge—instead.

The sun was making shadows that stretched across the hills and meadows by the time they looked down on the Colorado River. Along its red granite shore Tsena could see several hundred traveling tents and a few lodges. Columns of smoke arose from among them, filling the sky. Near the river in the center of this encampment stood the tall red lodge of Pochana Quoheep.

That evening Tsena walked through the camp toward the lodge, saying his words over and over. Everywhere warriors gathered to talk and smoke while women cooked at their fires.

The lower edge of Pochana Quoheep's lodge had been rolled up enough to let in the breeze but not prying eyes. Men's voices came from within. Outside, his small, pretty wife knelt by a fire putting hot stones in the stew.

"Good evening, wife of the chief of Twelve Bands," Tsena said.

She looked him over for a moment. "Are you not Tsena, son of the peace chief?"

He nodded. "I am Tsena Naku. I bring a message for the war chief."

She smiled. "He talks now with some of the chiefs, but they will soon smoke the pipe."

"Then I will wait," Tsena said and sat down on the other side of the door.

"Anawakeo has spoken of you," she said, looking sideways at him while stirring. "She says you acted as chief during your captivity—and very skillfully too."

Tsena looked down, flushing with pleasure. He longed to know what else Anawakeo had said. Instead he asked, "Her grandmother got home?"

"Yes, tired and weak, but Anawakeo nursed her back to health."

Soon Tsena heard the men stirring inside, and one by one they emerged from the opening. Isimanica glanced at him, frowned, but said nothing. *Does he guess why I am here?* Tsena wondered.

When everyone had gone, the chief's wife called, "Tsena Naku awaits you, my husband."

"Enter," came the command.

Tsena stepped inside. Pochana Quoheep sat opposite the door fanning himself, his wiry muscles bulging above the copper armlets he wore. He nodded and motioned for

191

him to sit. Tsena folded his legs, looking straight ahead, and waited for the chief to speak first. In the silence he felt Pochana Quoheep's eyes on him.

"You seek revenge for the death of your father." It was a statement, not a question.

Tsena looked at the chief then, at his lean, pocked face, his black-jewel eyes, and took a deep breath. "I have had my revenge, chief of the Twelve Bands. I come with words from Grandfather Ahsenap."

"Speak them."

"He believes our revenge should be an honorable one, equal to our loss—twelve scalps for twelve chiefs. Thus would we keep the lodge door open for peace. That is all."

The chief fanned himself and seemed to be looking into his own mind. His face showed no expression.

"Ahsenap is a wise man," he said at length, "but our loss is greater than he imagines." The crease between his eyebrows deepened. "Not only have we lost our great chiefs, but the northern bands—the Nokoni, the Kotsoteka, the Quohadi—they will not join us on the warpath. They think we do not have those things which the Great Spirit gave to men so that he could tell them from women." He paused, his jaws tight. "But we will show them."

Och, Tsena thought. *Even though the chief listened respectfully to Grandfather's words, he will never agree. The* Nemena *want revenge and he will lead them to it.*

Pochana Quoheep leaned back. "Now, tell me of your revenge. I have heard talk, but I would hear it from you."

Tsena nodded, pulled the pistol barrel from his belt, and told how he had taken it. He told of being a captive in the mission, his escape and vision, and his rescue by the messenger of the wolf. All the while Pochana Quoheep kept his eyes fastened on Tsena.

When he finished the chief said, "I like your observations, Tsena Naku. I suspect you have learned far more about the enemy than you tell. That could be of use to me. You see, to defeat the enemy we must understand him—otherwise we are the same as blind."

He reached out and placed his hand on Tsena's shoulder. "I want you to ride at my side on the warpath. And I want you to be my eyes and ears among the warriors."

The First Scalp

Two sleeps passed before warriors from all twelve
bands arrived. Tsena marveled at the great multitude.
There were five or six hundred at least, and with their
women and children the party probably numbered close
to a thousand. Never had there been such a war party.

It was the first day of the Moon when Buffalo
Bellow—the day of leaving. At first light Pochana
Quoheep's crier ran through the camp, calling, "When
Father Sun has risen one finger above the horizon,
gather around the sandy place." He stopped where Tsena
and Kianceta were folding up their buffalo hides. Tsena
looked over at him. He was a thin, intense boy and some-
what breathless.

"The chief of the Twelve Bands wishes you to assist him in the council meeting," he said, looking at Tsena. "You are to bring eight counting sticks."

Tsena nodded. "I will do so."

After he had ridden on, Kianceta said, "The chief honors you. He must like you for some reason." He gave Tsena a playful punch on the shoulder.

Tsena grinned. "He thinks I know something about the *tejanos*."

"He is right—you do."

"A little, but I wish I knew more," Tsena said, stuffing the hide in his saddle bag.

Kianceta nodded thoughtfully and began to pack his saddle bag. After a moment he looked back at Tsena. "Like what?"

"Like how to read Shakespeare's signs."

"What is that?" Kianceta asked, with a look on his face of tasting something bitter.

Tsena chuckled. The name did have a strange sound to it.

"Shakespeare was a wise man who lived three hundred winters ago, on the other side of the Great Water. He drew signs on paper that make words. Have you heard of white man's talking signs?"

"Yes, but I have never seen one."

"Come, I will show you if you help me find some sticks for the chief."

They walked away from the camp, up to a big liveoak

tree where there was a fallen branch. Tsena took out his knife, cut off a stick, and sharpened it. Then he wrote T-S-E-N-A in the dirt. "That says Tsena."

"Hmmmmm," Kianceta said. "It is not very pretty." He flashed his quick smile. "Why not just draw a wolf?"

"I could, but look, Ceta, I can use some of these signs to make other words—like your name." He paused, thinking how white man would write Ceta. It had some of the same sounds as Tsena.

Then he wrote S-E-T-A. "There . . . that says Ceta."

"It does?" Kianceta studied the signs, traced them with his finger. "I still like a picture of a weasel better than this."

"But how could you draw something Shakespeare said three hundred winters ago? Something like, 'If the past is bitter, more welcome is the sweet.'"

Kianceta's small, lively eyes widened. "I never would! That is for saying, not drawing."

"But white man has a way of drawing it so it will never be forgotten."

"*Och*, this makes me dizzy, Tsena. I don't want to know any more about white man. I just want him to go back where he came from."

Tsena nodded. He understood. Still, he could not forget his glimpse of another world. It would make him always different, like Lone Hill. Ceta was satisfied to know only his world. He did not understand the power white man had. He thought nothing would ever change. And, in a way, Tsena envied him.

He looked across the river where the first rays of the sun flashed over the treetops. It was time to finish cutting the sticks. Without another word, they set about the task.

When the sun had risen one finger, warriors assembled in a great circle. Pochana Quoheep strode to the center dressed only in a breechcloth, his lean, muscular body shining with bear grease.

"Today we start on the greatest warpath the *Nemena* have ever taken. The arrow of our trail will pierce deep into *tejano* territory—even to the Great Water." He looked around, seeming to engage each warrior with his glittering eyes. Then he stepped to the edge of the sandy place and began drawing a line.

"We will ride along the Colorado until it turns east." He marked the spot with a circle and motioned Tsena to plant the first counter for the first sleep.

As Tsena walked to the spot and pushed the stick into the sand, he was aware that all eyes were on him. He felt his heart swell, for it was an honor to be chosen for this job.

Pochana Quoheep continued drawing the warpath line, stopping for Tsena to mark the second and third sleeps. Then he drew two rivers, the Guadalupe and the Lavaca. "Between these rivers rises the Big Hill—the fourth sleep. From here we will ride with the rising moon so that our attack on the town they call Victoria will be a complete surprise."

Taking a few steps he drew the edge of land. "And here we come to Linnville—our final strike." He straightened himself and looked around. "Commit this map to memory, brave warriors. We shall revenge the massacre of our chiefs. That is all."

For three days the great war party moved over the rolling hills to the southeast, while Father Sun bore down on them with all his heat. Tsena rode beside Pochana Quoheep in the lead. Sweat poured from his body and he longed for water, but he knew they would not stop to drink until they made camp. This was the warpath.

On the third day as the sun set, Pochana Quoheep pointed ahead. "The Big Hill."

Tsena saw that it was not like Lone Hill. Here nothing stood alone—the land rolled and was covered with grass. The Big Hill was simply the highest roll.

At a creek that ran beside the hill the chief halted and called Wutsuki to him. "We will camp here until the moon rises tomorrow night," he said. "Go and spread the word."

Later, when Tsena and Kianceta had drunk their fill and bathed in the creek, they ate some pemmican and lay down to sleep among the warriors of their village. A cooling breeze swept along the creek bed, and Tsena stretched out, listening to the murmur of voices all around.

Soon Kianceta was drawing deep breaths of sleep. The camp quieted, the small fires were put out, but Tsena lay awake. Nearby one fire still glowed. He rolled over on his side and watched the group of warriors sitting with Isimanica, including Kiyou. They spoke so quietly that he could not hear their words. Presently they nodded in agreement and settled down to sleep. What did it mean?

The next morning when Tsena awoke at first light, he saw that Isimanica and his warriors were gone. This was something Pochana Quoheep needed to know.

Kianceta still slept like a small boy, curled up on the hide, but the rest of the camp was beginning to stir. Noiselessly, Tsena arose and hurried along the creek to the chief's red lodge.

"Chief of the Twelve Bands, it is Tsena Naku. May I enter?"

"Yes, enter."

The chief and his wife sat eating the first meal of the day.

"You wish me to be your eyes and ears, and last night I saw Chief Isimanica talking with several warriors around his fire. I could not hear their words, but this morning they are gone."

Pochana Quoheep frowned, motioning him to sit. His

wife offered Tsena strips of dried meat and persimmons. They ate in silence while the chief pondered.

At last he said, "I suspect Isimanica has gone in search of the first scalp." He shook his head slowly from side to side. "He pricks me as if he had porcupine quills. This could ruin our surprise attack."

There was a pause, then he went on. "It seems to me that Isimanica would lead this war party himself. What do you say, Tsena Naku? You know him well."

"I think he cares only for his own glory."

The chief nodded. "I think you speak truly. He will never make a great leader, but he could divide the war party." He put a hand on Tsena's shoulder. "Thank you for bringing me the news, my eyes and ears. It gives me time to decide how to deal with a porcupine."

The sun was halfway down the sky when Tsena heard horses coming. He hurried along the creek bank, weaving in and out among the small tents and groups of warriors, until he reached Pochana Quoheep's lodge. The chief stood watching the party approach. Isimanica led them straight to the red lodge and reined in at full gallop.

Tsena looked them over. He saw the triumph on their faces as Isimanica raised a bloody scalp on the tip of an arrow. "The first scalp!" he shouted. "I have taken the first *tejano* scalp. The war of revenge has begun. It is good medicine."

Is it? Tsena wondered. *This could ruin the surprise attack.*

"We encountered two of them traveling along a road and gave chase," Isimanica went on. "My nephew counted coup on one, and Pakawa put an arrow in his side."

The warriors yipped.

Kiyou sat on his horse beside his uncle holding the reins of another horse, a fine long-legged black. He looked down at Tsena, grinning.

"The other *tejano* rode a fast horse," Isimanica said, "but we overtook him, and now his scalp and his horse are mine." Isimanica raised his arms in triumph.

All around Tsena, warriors yelled, *"Aieeeee, aieeeee, aieeeee!"*

Pochana Quoheep waited for silence, his jaw tensed. *What will he say?* Tsena wondered. *How will he show everyone that he still leads this war party?*

When the crowd had quieted, he put his hands on his hips and spoke, measuring his words. "Where is the other scalp?"

Tsena saw that Isimanica could not meet the chief's eyes. He turned away and looked at the stolen horse.

"We did not stop to take it," he said then, "but pursued the one who rode this horse instead—a prize far greater than another scalp."

There was a long silence while Pochana Quoheep

studied him. Isimanica could not remain still. He patted his horse and glanced around at the warriors.

"Was the other *tejano* dead?" Pochana Quoheep asked then.

Isimanica frowned. "Do you think I am like a puppy only five sleeps old? Do you think I would let a *tejano* live to tell his story?"

After a brief silence the chief repeated his question. "Was he dead?"

"Yes, may Father Sun strike me down if I speak falsely."

Pochana Quoheep nodded. "So be it."

How ominous those three words sounded. Like the call of an owl. Tsena did not believe Isimanica had told the truth, and apparently neither did Pochana Quoheep.

Before dawn of the sixth sleep they came to a creek north of the town of Victoria, and Pochana Quoheep halted. They had ridden all night by the moon.

"Go, Wutsuki," he said, "tell the women to make camp here. And you, Tsena Naku, rest a while and come to my lodge when the sun is five fingers above the horizon."

Even though his body was heavy with weariness, Tsena slept fitfully. He worried that once he fell asleep he would not wake up until too late.

He kept jerking awake and measuring the sun's distance with his fingers. Between four and five he roused himself, washed his face, and walked through the camp to the red lodge.

"I have summoned your brother as well," said the chief. "I want the two of you to ride ahead and look over the town."

"You honor me, chief of the Twelve Bands. But even though Kiyou is my brother . . . he is also like a porcupine."

"So," said the chief, nodding. He leaned closer. "Today you and I will soothe the porcupine and flatten his quills." He leaned back and grinned.

Kiyou soon came. He glanced aside at Tsena for a moment with an arrogant look and sat down where the chief motioned him.

After he explained the scouting mission, the chief said, "Take care you are not seen. I want to know whether they are expecting an attack. Now go . . . and watch out for porcupines."

Tsena saw the twitch at the corner of the chief's mouth to keep from smiling. *Kiyou must wonder what he meant. Let him wonder.*

They rode to the south, side by side, without speaking. Finally, Kiyou asked, "What did he mean about porcupines? Did he have another vision?"

"He does not tell me his visions."

"But you are favored by him, Grandmother."

Tsena's jaw tightened. *Soothe the porcupine*, he thought. Turning, he looked squarely at Kiyou and said slowly, "Do not call me that again."

Kiyou only shrugged.

Approaching a rise, they stopped and looked at

each other. As if by silent consent, they dismounted and crawled to the top. The town of Victoria lay on a broad plain beside the Guadalupe River. A large herd of horses—several hundred—grazed peacefully nearby.

"The men of this town are wealthy," Tsena said quietly.

"And stupid," said Kiyou. "They leave their horses unguarded. They cannot imagine we would come this far."

Tsena said nothing. Kiyou was right about the last part—the town was completely unguarded. From this distance he could see only a few people—a woman working in her garden, children playing in the street. Smoke rose from chimneys and hung over the town in the hot, still air. In a planted field to the east four black-skinned men chopped at the ground.

"Buffalo men," said Kiyou. "I guess you love them too like you love *tejanos*."

Something let go inside Tsena. He jerked his head around, and the words came spilling out. "I will tell you this, Kiyou. I hate the *tejanos* who killed our chiefs. But I do not hate all of them. There are good ones and bad ones—just as there are among us."

Kiyou's mouth opened, but he said nothing. Tsena looked away at Victoria, and they talked no more.

When they returned to camp, Pochana Quoheep was sitting with the other chiefs in a circle. They passed the pipe in silence. Tsena and Kiyou stood with the other warriors, waiting until Pochana Quoheep motioned them to enter the circle.

"Tell us, Tsena Naku, what do you think of this town?"

Tsena nodded once. "They suspect nothing, chief of the Twelve Bands. Children play and women work in their gardens."

Then Pochana Quoheep turned to Kiyou. As the boy told about the hundreds of horses grazing on the plain, the warriors began to stir and talk among themselves.

"It will be a raid our grandchildren will tell their grandchildren about," said one of the chiefs after Kiyou had finished.

Pochana Quoheep frowned. "We come here on a war of revenge, not a horse raid," he said. "If we burden ourselves with horses, our return will be slow and our trail marked by a great cloud of dust—easily followed even by *tejanos*. What say the rest of you?"

Tsena looked around the circle and saw Isimanica stand up and fold his arms over his fat chest. "I say there will be no *tejanos* left to see our dust. Their hearts will all sleep. Let us take both scalps and horses."

Others nodded agreement. One of the warriors, a Kiowa, said, "Surely with our great numbers we can take what we please—unless we are women!"

Pochana Quoheep listened, his mouth clamped shut, as others spoke in favor of taking the horses. After all who wished had spoken, there was a long silence. *What will the war chief say?* Tsena wondered. It was his vision, his medicine that had sent them off on this warpath. Now he seemed to be losing control.

He stood and took his time looking around the circle. "I would not deny the desire of brave warriors to take horses." Then he focused on Isimanica. "You, Isimanica, and your band will drive the horses back here while we surround the town."

Isimanica frowned. "But my warriors cannot count coup on horses."

"There will be other opportunities for counting coup before we turn back, but only this opportunity for capturing a vast herd. You want horses—now is the time to take them. I have spoken."

Instead of soothing the porcupine, Pochana Quoheep's words were causing the quills to rise on Isimanica's back. Tsena saw him look around to see what others thought.

But Pochana Quoheep was finished with the subject. "Now," he said, "tie up the tails of your horses and assemble below the rise. When I raise my shield, move to the crest. And when I raise my bow—attack! We will show them how the *Nemena* revenge their chiefs."

Panic rose in Tsena's throat. His first attack. Would he bring honor to himself or shame? Would his wolf medicine protect him from bullets?

As Pochana Quoheep mounted his horse, he turned

to Tsena. "Stay with me and you will come to no harm. You are a novice—watch the other warriors and learn."

Tsena nodded once, grateful to the chief for seeming to know how he felt.

At the rise warriors formed into a long line on either side of the war chief. They were painted, armed with bows and lances, shields in place. The horses snorted and tossed their heads. Tsena touched his medicine bag. The stone and tuft of fur were there. *Spirit Wolf, go with me*, he prayed silently. Then he took out his bow and one arrow and adjusted Grandfather's shield.

Pochana Quoheep raised his shield, and they moved up to the crest. Tsena's heart began to race. The buffalo men were still working in the field. They did not yet know that six hundred warriors were about to ride down upon them.

Attack!

When Pochana Quoheep raised his bow, the line
bolted forward. Warriors yipped and screamed above
thundering hooves, and, in spite of himself, the sound
stirred Tsena's blood. Yuaneh stretched out her legs and
gobbled up the ground. The wind of their speed flowed
over his body, cooling him like water. The buffalo men
straightened up and, for a moment, stood watching.
Then they turned and fled, leaping over rows of plants.
Closer and closer came the line of warriors.

They were right upon the running men now. One
glanced over his shoulder, then stopped and crouched
down in the leaves directly in their path. Pochana
Quoheep veered to go around them, motioning Tsena to

follow. A warrior on Tsena's other side shouted, *"Ahey!"* He lowered his lance and drove it through the buffalo man with all the force of his speed.

A howl split the air. Tsena looked back and saw the warrior pull his horse up into a rearing halt. The buffalo man jerked about, pinned to the ground by the lance.

Suddenly, Tsena was trembling. He twisted his fingers into Yuaneh's mane and let the wind wash over him while his mare galloped on, carrying him with her.

When they neared the town, Pochana Quoheep raised one arm and made a circular motion. He led the way around Victoria as the yipping warriors fell in behind him.

A few *tejanos* gathered at the edge of town. Puffs of smoke exploded from their long guns. Arrows flew through the air. Tsena pulled back his bowstring, aimed, and let his arrow fly, though where it hit he did not know. One *tejano* fell back, clutching at the arrow in his shoulder. Was it his?

By the time Tsena and the chief circled the town, all the *tejanos* had fled into their stone lodges and bolted the doors. It seemed they were not going to fight. Two lay on the ground at the edge of town. Warriors broke from the circle and rushed in. The first to strike coup shouted, *"Ahey!"* Two others leaped from their horses and began taking the scalps.

Tsena galloped on, following the chief in a circle that was getting smaller each time around the town. The two warriors rejoined the circle with bloody scalps held high on their lances, yipping and yelling. It was no surprise that the *tejanos* did not come out. Arrows could never penetrate those stone walls.

"Stay inside," Tsena yelled, amidst the noise of pounding hooves and yipping. As he came around the west side of town he saw Isimanica and his warriors herding the horses north toward camp. How clever of Pochana Quoheep to give him the task of taking horses.

At last the chief of the Twelve Bands broke the circle and signaled for everyone to gather around. "Their roofs are made of wood," he said. "Tomorrow we will return with fire and force them out. Now let us retire and make ready."

Tsena leaned back and let his breath out. It was over for today. They had taken two scalps. Would they take ten more or a hundred before returning?

They headed north toward camp following the great herd of horses. If only they could keep on going to their villages in the hills, taking the horses as revenge enough. But revenge was not taken in horses, Tsena knew, only in scalps.

Back in camp, Isimanica swaggered up to Pochana Quoheep, hands on hips. "If I had ridden in the circle, the walls of the town would be spattered with *tejano* blood now, and we would have many scalps—not just two."

Pochana Quoheep studied him for a moment. Then he spoke quietly. "Your time will come, Isimanica."

Once again there was that ominous sound to Pochana Quoheep's words. What did he mean? That Isimanica would get his scalps? Or that he would be killed by the *tejanos*?

That night, as Tsena and Kianceta lay down to sleep near the creek, they could hear the snorting and occasional whinny from the herd.

"So many horses," said Kianceta. "Is this a war of revenge or a raid?"

"Pochana Quoheep is wondering the same thing." Tsena rolled over on his side to face his friend. "And trying to keep Isimanica from taking control of this war party. If he had not let the warriors take horses, he might have lost it."

"That is true," said Kianceta. "I would not like being in his place."

"Neither would I, but I think there is something worse to worry about."

"Like getting back alive?"

"Yes. The *tejanos* are not going to keep on hiding in their stone lodges. I think they are going to attack."

"But we outnumber them," said Kianceta.

"We do now, but maybe not for long."

Kianceta sat up suddenly. "What do you mean?"

Tsena also sat up and whispered. "I think Isimanica let a *tejano* escape back at the Big Hill. It is not like him to leave an enemy's scalp on his head. And if that is so . . . they could be gathering to attack us even now."

"But he swore an oath. He will be struck down if he lied."

"So be it," Tsena added.

At first light Wutsuki went around the camp, crying, "Arise, novice warriors, and gather moss to make torches. You will carry the fire. So says the chief of the Twelve Bands."

Tsena opened his eyes. It was a relief to know that all he had to do was carry fire. He did not have to kill anyone or take a scalp. He only had to carry fire.

Beside him Kianceta sat up and jabbed playfully at Tsena. "Arise, great warrior, and gather moss!"

As Kianceta stood, Tsena rolled over, grabbed him around the legs, and pulled him down. They wrestled about, and for a moment Tsena forgot where they were and why.

Then a pair of moccasined feet came and planted themselves in a wide stance. Tsena did not have to look up to know it was Isimanica.

"You heard the crier—this is no time for play," he said in his deep voice.

Tsena felt his face burn with shame. He scrambled up and nodded briefly to Isimanica. The chief turned and stalked away. Tsena glanced at Kianceta, and without a word they went to gather moss and find two strong branches. *What was I thinking?* Tsena wondered as they walked along. *Acting like a child when I am supposed to be a man.*

They found a liveoak with moss hanging from its branches and set to work. Somehow the making of torches—the careful winding and tying of the moss to the end of each stick—helped ease his shame. He was doing what the chief had ordered him to do.

When the torches were ready and the women had taken down the tents and loaded them onto the pack horses, the warriors assembled around Pochana Quoheep.

"We will circle the town as before," he said. "There is a coup for anyone whose arrow starts a fire." He glanced at Tsena. "Torch bearers are to ride in the circle and be ready to light arrows. That is all." He strode to his horse, mounted, and led the way out of camp.

As warriors lined up on the crest north of town, women brought fire to each torch bearer. Yuaneh looked around at the flaming torch and stepped sideways nervously.

Tsena patted her neck. "Trust me, little mare."

As soon as the torches were lit, Pochana Quoheep gave the signal. They charged down from the rise, trailing smoke and screaming, *"Aieeeee, aieeeee!"* Tsena rode, clutching his torch as the wind tried to snatch it away. From the corner of his eye he caught sight of four *tejanos* galloping toward Victoria from the east. One rode a mule and lagged behind. They all leaned low over their mounts and rode for their lives.

Warriors on the left flank shot forward, heading for the *tejanos*. One warrior overtook the mule rider and drove his lance through the man's body. Arrows flew, and a second man fell. The other two rode hard for town. Tsena watched them as Yuaneh galloped on. More than anything he wanted them to escape. *Hurry*, he thought, *hurry!*

Suddenly, gunfire and smoke erupted from the windows of a lodge at the edge of town. The warriors reined in, and the *tejanos* galloped on to safety. At least for the moment, Tsena thought.

Pochana Quoheep gave the signal to circle. Tsena followed him, holding out his torch as warriors rode alongside and touched the tips of their arrows to the fire. Smoke and war cries swirled around him. He saw warriors ride in closer to the town and loose their flaming arrows. He saw the arrows fall on roofs and catch fire. Even so, the *tejanos* kept up their gunfire. Warriors circled, yelling and shooting, but they could not enter the streets.

Finally, Pochana Quoheep broke the circle and motioned to the east where the women waited. The yelling died down and warriors followed him and gathered around. Behind them Victoria burned, sending up dark smoke.

"We have punished this town," Pochana Quoheep shouted. "Now on to the Great Water."

The Book

They camped that night on Placedo Creek. Tsena stretched out on his buffalo hide and looked up at the bulging moon. A sea breeze sent clouds racing across it. He thought about Spirit Wolf and the night of his vision. "The white wolves come running, behold them and listen," he sang softly, over and over. *Why does Spirit Wolf not answer?* he wondered. *Have I offended him?*

Suddenly, a baby's cry pierced the air. Tsena raised up on one elbow. *Nemena* babies never cried out in the night. It was the white baby, of course. Its mother sat tied around the waist to a tree, cradling the baby in her arms.

Isimanica got up and strode to her. "Silence," he

215

demanded with his hands on his hips. She began to rock back and forth and sing in a shaky voice. Gradually, with little whimpers, the crying ceased.

Earlier that day Isimanica had taken them captive. Not long after leaving Victoria, the party had come upon a lone farmhouse and set it afire. As the flames leaped to the sky a woman rushed out, carrying a baby in her arms, and ran for a nearby creek. Isimanica rode her down. She fell to the ground, shielding the baby with her body. He dismounted and flung himself on her as the baby screamed. Tsena watched—though it filled him with disgust.

Now a creeping dread came over him. If the baby cried again it would die. He was sure of that. He looked over at Kianceta, who slept as soundly as if they were back in the village. Tsena closed his eyes and listened to the tree frogs singing back and forth across the creek—a sleepy sound. He hoped it would lull the baby to sleep. For a long time he lay there with his arms and legs tensed. Then slowly, slowly he felt himself sinking into darkness.

He awoke to Wutsuki's voice, first in the distance and now close by. "Arise, warriors, we depart before dawn."

Tsena opened his eyes. The moon had set, and there was a faint glow on the horizon toward the Great Water. Today he would see it for the first time—the end of land, the beginning of water. And then they would turn back.

He stretched and sat up. Dark forms moved about the camp taking down tents, packing up belongings.

When all was ready, Tsena mounted Yuaneh and took his place beside the chief at the head of the procession. The other chiefs lined up on either side. At that moment the baby started crying again. Tsena looked back. Its mother, her legs tied to a trail horse behind Isimanica, put the baby to her breast. But it continued to cry, its tiny arms waving about in rage.

Isimanica jerked his horse around. "Make it stop or I *will!*" he bellowed.

The baby stopped for a moment and looked at him. Then it turned away and began to scream. The mother clutched it close and muffled the cries against her breast, jostling it frantically.

Isimanica ripped the baby from her arms and flung it to the ground like a bag of sand. As the mother reached out her arms, screaming "*No-o-o-o-o!*" he drove his lance into it.

Tsena felt his insides rise up into his throat. He leaned over and retched. Then he spat and wiped his mouth. The white woman screamed until Isimanica hit her with the side of his lance and she slumped over the horse.

Pochana Quoheep raised his bow and the procession started off. Yuaneh moved along without any signal. Tsena wanted to turn about and ride for the hills. If this was their glorious revenge, he wanted no part of it. Yet there was no escape. He was being swept along in a river toward the Great Water.

"The stomach has to come up once before it is hardened to battle," Pochana Quoheep said quietly. "It was so with me."

Tsena said nothing. This was not a battle—it was the killing of a helpless baby.

"I was sixteen winters when I took my first scalp," he went on. "And my stomach came up. Even now it is not hard enough to kill a baby."

Tsena looked at the chief then, at the grim expression on his pocked face. *He does not like what Isimanica did either, and for that I will ride at his side until this warpath is over.*

The chief pointed ahead where the tip of the sun flashed over the horizon. "The Old Ones say that journeying east at dawn brings good fortune. I hope they are right."

Tsena hoped so too. Yet the dread was still there.

After they had ridden silently for a way, the chief said, "It troubles me that all these horses slow us down. Do you think the *tejanos* will pursue us?"

"Yes, chief of the Twelve Bands, when they find we have taken one of their women and killed a child. Women and children are sacred to them—more sacred than horses."

Pochana Quoheep straightened his shoulders and looked ahead. A muscle in his jaw clenched. "Our women and children—and chiefs—are sacred too. Do the *tejanos* not understand that?"

"They understand little about us," Tsena said.

Coming to the top of a rise, Tsena saw the Great Water in the distance. He stared at the sight. The water glistened and swam about under the red sun, and a ship with white wings floated upon it. But there was no time to marvel as they drew closer to the small town at the edge of the water.

Pochana Quoheep made a sign for the warriors to form a line on either side. "Stay with me, Tsena Naku," he said. He raised his bow, and the warriors surged forward, shrieking.

People ran out of their lodges and gathered on the low embankment. Then they began to wade out into the water and climb into small boats. By the time Tsena followed Pochana Quoheep between lodges to the edge of the embankment, the *tejanos* were rowing out to sea, out of arrow range. The chief reined in and Tsena halted beside him. They watched as warriors rode down the bank and splashed into the water, waving war clubs and bows and shouting, "Go back across the water! Go back where you came from!"

At that moment a *tejano* emerged from one of the lodges, pulling a red-haired woman by the hand. As they ran for the water, warriors overtook them, and one split the man's head with his war club. Others jumped from their horses and grabbed the woman. She pounded them with her fists and kicked. Suddenly, her long red hair flew loose. The warriors fell back, as if stunned by her strange fair beauty.

Tsena sucked in his breath and held it. What would they do to her? Then a warrior reached out and ripped off her dress, leaving only her white underclothes and a stiff garment laced to her body. Another warrior grabbed her arms, pinning them to her side. She screamed at them and flung her hair about like a flame of fire.

"Enough!" shouted Pochana Quoheep. "Tie her up."

Everything stopped. The warriors turned at the sound of the chief's voice. The woman stopped struggling and stared at him. Out in the bay, *tejanos* watched solemnly.

"Let them see that we respect such beauty," said Pochana Quoheep, motioning toward the people in the boats.

Tsena looked at him with admiration. It took courage to deny warriors the use of a captive woman. But the woman did not realize that. She began to thrash about again as the warriors bound her arms and legs. Only when she was tied across a horse did she cease fighting and seem to droop.

The crack of splintering wood made Tsena turn away. Isimanica and other warriors had broken open the door of a long wooden lodge and entered. Then, one by one, they came out carrying strips of cloth, ribbons of all colors, and white man's clothing. Isimanica came swaggering out the door wearing a tall black hat and carrying a sunshade. He mounted his horse and pranced about, twirling the sunshade over his head. Kiyou stepped out in a black coat tied at the waist with a strip of red cloth.

Then Kianceta burst from the doorway, leaped on his horse, and came trotting over to Tsena. He held up streamers of ribbons that whipped about in the wind. "For our horses!" he cried, giving a handful to Tsena.

All around them warriors rode back and forth through the town, shouting and laughing, trailing strips of red cloth. They ripped open pillows, and feathers flew everywhere. A few chased stray cows and pigs and drove their lances into them for sport.

Tsena forgot the *tejanos* in the boats, the red-haired woman, the baby. He dismounted and took the ribbons that Kianceta handed him. Yuaneh stepped nervously to the side. Tsena put his hand on her mane. "You will look beautiful, my little mare. Trust me." She stood still while he tied ribbons to her mane and tail. Then he saw a strip of red cloth blowing across the ground and ran to pick it up. "For us, Ceta," he shouted, "a sash." He tore the cloth in two long pieces, gave one to his friend, and tied the other around his waist.

They galloped along the embankment side by side. Other warriors rode down the bank and into the bay, sending sprays of water high into the air. They screamed and wheeled their horses around. Tsena saw a *tejano* leap out of a boat and start wading toward shore. He was yelling and waving a long gun over his head.

"Stay away from him!" Tsena shouted. "He has strong medicine." They rode up the embankment, into town, and stopped. Looking back, Tsena saw one of the boats move near the *tejano*, and he climbed in.

By now the women had reached the town. Tsena watched them run out of lodges carrying pots and pans, blankets, kegs of firewater, bags of tobacco, barrel hoops, clothing. Pochana Quoheep's wife had slipped a red ruffled skirt over her dress and was tying some pots to her saddle.

Nearby Tsena saw a small black book on the ground, its gold-edged pages fluttering in the wind. Quickly he dismounted and picked it up. "Look, Ceta, this is better than hats or coats or tobacco."

Suddenly, a page came loose and blew away. Forgetting all else Tsena ran and caught it and carefully placed it in the book. On the cover were two short words written in gold signs: *THE ILIAD*. He recognized signs he had learned to write. There was a *T* and *E* and *A*, the same signs as in his name, *I* and *L* as in Will's name, *H* and *D* as in HORSE and DOG. But he could not read these new words.

While he studied the signs, Yuaneh came and nudged his arm. He looked up at her and tucked the book in his red sash. A few paces away Pochana Quoheep sat on his horse, watching everything with a grim expression

222

on his face. There were no ribbons tied to his horse, no hat on his head.

"Tsena Naku," he called and jerked his head upward.

Tsena walked toward the chief slowly with his mare following. He was ashamed of the sash and Yuaneh's ribbons—but not of the book. He would keep it for all his days.

"Look at them," said Pochana Quoheep disgustedly. "They would take it all—pots, cloth, skirts. My own wife dresses like a white woman. Even you have forgotten yourself."

Tsena felt his face flush, but he clutched the book. No one—not even the chief—could make him give it up.

"What will you do with white man's signs? Can you read them?"

"Only a little, chief of the Twelve Bands. But I shall learn, for they have great power."

Pochana Quoheep looked at him for a moment and nodded. "Keep it, if you wish, Tsena Naku. Perhaps you are right." He breathed in sharply and waved an arm around at the others. "But it will take a moon to get home with all these horses loaded with white man's things."

Tsena kept his silence. He knew the chief was right.

When at last there was no place for another pot or pan, Pochana Quoheep ordered fire set to every lodge. The *tejanos* watched from their boats. Now and then one would stand and shout something, only to be pulled down by others.

As fires blazed, Pochana Quoheep raised his bow and the chiefs gathered around. "Our revenge is done," he said. "Now let us start back."

He led the procession out of the burning town. Tsena looked back once, but he could not see the Great Water, for the whole coastline was burning.

The Battle

Under a blazing sun the procession snaked its way slowly northwest across the coastal prairie, onto the rolling land, and over the Big Hill. Dust rose up from the horses' hooves into a towering cloud. It coated Tsena's face and body and clogged his throat. He was riding Yuaneh today, and she too was covered with dust. The brightly colored ribbons were dirty and limp now.

For three sleeps a small group of *tejanos* had been following them. Several times fighting broke out in the rear and forced them to move a little faster. With all the heavy loot, some of the mules lagged behind. Pochana Quoheep ordered them shot rather than let the *tejanos* have them.

"Never have I returned from the warpath at such a

pace," Pochana Quoheep said, looking straight ahead and scowling. "What began as a noble war of revenge has turned into a pots and pans raid."

"Could you not tell them to leave it all behind?" Tsena asked.

"Yes, I could do that, but never again would warriors follow me. They want horses and ridiculous hats. And our women want skirts and pots." He heaved a sigh and looked at Tsena. "No, we must continue like turtles and hope the *tejanos* give up and go home."

Cicadas buzzed all around—a drowsy sound that matched their slow pace. Still, Yuaneh swiveled her ears from side to side and pranced nervously. Tsena had to keep a tight rein. Did she sense danger?

Just as darkness was falling the chief decided to stop for the night in a grove of liveoaks. Guards were posted all around, a few fires were lit, and people spread hides on the ground under the moon. The beautiful red-haired woman sat leaning against a tree, not far from Pochana Quoheep's fire and not far from the place where Tsena and Kianceta had spread their buffalo hides.

No warrior had touched her during the long journey—not even Isimanica. *Maybe because Pochana Quoheep is saving her for himself*, thought Tsena. Or maybe because there was something sacred about her. Her skin glowed like the moon itself, cool and white. And her long hair burned like fire. If anyone came near, she flung it from side to side. He longed to ask her about the book he had picked up, especially about the picture of the huge wooden horse with warriors coming out of its side.

Now on the fourth night she had calmed down and began to look around the camp. Maybe this was the time, Tsena thought. Pulling the book from his sash, he said, "Come with me, Ceta. I am going to ask the red-haired woman to read aloud from my book."

Kianceta looked at him as if he were crazy, but he came along. They walked to the tree where she sat, and Tsena held the book out to her. She watched him, her face expressionless.

"Shakespeare?" he asked.

Her mouth opened. She took the book in both hands and glanced at the cover.

"No Shakespeare," she said, shaking her head.

"*Qué lástima*," Tsena said. He paused, staring at the book.

"*Iliad*," she said.

"Il–ee–ahd?" he repeated.

She nodded. "*Sí*, very old story."

"How many years?"

"Three . . . how do you say?" She looked up at the moon as if an answer would come from there. "Thousand. *Sí*, it has three thousand years."

"Three thousand?"

"*Sí*, a story about a war and . . . and a woman."

"And a horse of wood?"

227

"*Sí*, a horse of wood where soldiers hide. Then they come out and fight."

"I want you to read some," Tsena said.

She nodded once and opened the book. "*Comprende* English?" she asked.

Tsena shook his head. "No, but I like to hear the words."

She motioned for them to sit down. Then she turned the book toward the firelight, and began to read. White man's words tumbled from her mouth. Other warriors came and sat around her. Though no one understood, they listened.

The words were about a war three thousand winters ago. Tsena wondered if any of them told about a young warrior's stomach coming up. And if the woman in that story had red hair too. Would someone write words about Pochana Quoheep's pots and pans raid so that three thousand winters from now someone else could read it? If only he could write words.

Much later that night, while the camp slept, Tsena was awakened by a wolf howling in the distance. His heart leaped. Could it be Spirit Wolf? He walked out into the meadow, raised his arms to the moon, and sang.

> "*The white wolves come running,*
> *The white wolves come running.*
> *Behold them and listen,*
> *Behold them and speak.*"

He sat down in the moon path. Would the wolf call to him or give him a sign? For a long time he sat in the meadow. The air was hot and still. His eyes closed and his head slumped forward. As the dark robe of sleep came over him, he heard himself drawing deep breaths.

A wolf howled, closer this time. Tsena's head was so heavy he could not lift it or open his eyes. But behind his eyes he saw Spirit Wolf standing in the moon path, his white fur shining. He raised his muzzle to the sky.

"Hear me, Tsena Naku, danger awaits in the east. Be watchful on the morrow and do not ride Yuaneh. She is wise and knows the way."

Spirit Wolf stood there a moment longer, his white plume of a tail moving slowly from side to side. Then he turned and leaped up the moon path.

Tsena awoke with a start. There was no wolf, only the moon and its empty path. But Spirit Wolf had spoken to him, and Tsena would heed his words—even though he did not understand. He could not help wondering why he should not ride Yuaneh, especially if there was danger. And what did the wolf mean by saying, *she is wise and knows the way*? He roused himself and walked back to camp. *Trust your medicine*, he told himself.

People were beginning to stir even though there was not the slightest glow in the east. Tsena went directly to the place where Pochana Quoheep had spent the night. The chief stood watching him approach while his wife loaded the pack mule.

Will he take the wolf's words seriously? Tsena wondered. His medicine was still new and untested. But he was the chief's eyes and ears, and he would report everything he saw and heard and dreamed.

"May I tell you about a dream?" Tsena asked.

"Yes, of course."

Tsena moved closer and whispered, "Spirit Wolf came to me and said that danger awaits us today. He told me to watch the east."

Pochana Quoheep nodded. "Then you must do so, riding at my side."

Before dawn the long procession was once again mounted and moving. Tsena rode his trail horse beside Pochana Quoheep and kept his eyes toward the east. Yuaneh followed along on a tether and occasionally pranced up beside him and nuzzled his leg.

"My wise little mare." He stroked her forehead, keeping watch as Father Sun glinted through the trees.

It was soon after they crossed a creek and came onto a broad flat meadow that he caught sight of movement in the trees bordering the creek. Squinting his eyes, he looked hard into the shadows. What he saw sent a stab of alarm through his body and set his heart racing. Men— many of them—wearing hats.

"Chief of the Twelve Bands, look to the east," he whispered. *"Tejanos."*

Slowly, Pochana Quoheep turned his head. "I see them."

He motioned Wutsuki to come up beside him. "Go and tell the chiefs to choose their bravest warriors and ride out between us and the *tejanos* to the east. Distract them until we can get the women and horses safely past." He glanced at Tsena then, nodding his thanks.

Soon the warriors galloped out into the meadow. They were still painted for war. Some wore buffalo horns, others their tall black hats, and two Kiowas wore feather head-dresses. The horses, painted with lightning signs and coup marks, pranced and wheeled about. Ribbons in their manes and tails fluttered in the wind of their going. Tsena watched, hoping the *tejanos* were fooled by this bluff.

But they were not. They came out of the woods and followed the procession. Tsena looked back. So many! Perhaps two hundred mounted *tejanos* with their long guns. Even some Tonkawas on foot.

There was no choice but to turn and fight so the women could get away. If only he were on Yuaneh. She trotted along beside him, but he dared not slip onto her back. He glanced at Pochana Quoheep. What would he do now?

When they reached a clump of oak trees on the other side of the meadow, the chief halted and turned to Wutsuki, who had returned. "Tell the warriors to gather here to guard the women. And tell the women to keep on driving the herd."

The boy nodded and rode back through the long procession spreading the word.

"Mount your war horse and stay by me," Pochana Quoheep said to Tsena.

Trust your medicine, Tsena told himself. He stayed at the chief's side but let go of Yuaneh's tether. Strangely, she trotted off and broke into a gallop. *She is wise and knows the way*, Spirit Wolf had said. Was she heading home without him?

"Why do you let her go?" asked Pochana Quoheep.

"Because of my dream."

The chief nodded as he watched the procession pass by. Warriors gathered around him while those out in the meadow continued to prance about on their horses in front of the *tejanos*.

Slowly, the *tejanos* advanced. Then they stopped, dismounted, and formed into lines.

"Why do they dismount?" Pochana Quoheep asked.

"They are about to kneel and start firing—it is white man's way."

"Then we shall fight them in our way." The chief turned to Tsena. "You stay here with the rear guard." Then he galloped out toward the prancing warriors, making the sign of a circle as he went. Isimanica rode out too, wearing his tall black hat, his medicine shield on one arm, his bow in hand.

Tsena watched the warriors begin to ride around the *tejanos* in a magic circle—out of range of their long guns. They yelled, "*Aieeeee, aieeeee,*" and let their arrows fly.

The *tejanos* did not look impressed. They knew nothing of the magic circle or a medicine shield. They knew only the magic of their long guns. They knelt and aimed. Tsena was seized with dread. *Is the magic of their guns stronger than ours?*

Isimanica broke from the circle and approached them. "I challenge one of you to come out and fight." He raised his bow above his head. "I will show you how *Nemena* kill *tejanos!*" They fired their guns, but their bullets did not hit him.

"See, my uncle has the strongest medicine of all," Kiyou shouted as he watched from nearby.

Isimanica pranced his horse closer. He seemed sure of his medicine. He thrust his shield high above his head and shouted, "Your bullets cannot kill me!"

Several shots cracked. He slumped forward, slipping to the ground.

Tsena moaned. It was bad medicine. All around him a low moan filled the air. He watched as Pochana Quoheep broke the circle, and the warriors began to flee in all directions. Two of them galloped to Isimanica, but before they could reach down to grab his arms, they were hit by bullets. At that moment Kiyou and another warrior galloped out to his uncle, took hold of his arms, and dragged him back. But the breath of life had left his huge, limp body, and he lay bleeding from a chest wound. Tsena stared down at him, unable to move.

Then the *tejanos* shouted. They were running to their horses, leaping astride, their long guns in hand. All at once they bolted forward, riding hard for the clump of oaks where Tsena and the other warriors were guarding the retreat.

Pochana Quoheep galloped by, shouting to Tsena, "Follow me."

Tsena jerked Nooki about and kicked him hard in the ribs. He lost sight of the chief in the press of fleeing warriors all around him—so close that he could turn neither right nor left. Suddenly, they were upon the herd which had come to a standstill. To his horror Tsena saw that the horses and pack mules were struggling in a boggy marsh, unable to move. Horses whinnied and women screamed as the *tejanos* thundered closer.

And now he and the warriors were caught in the writhing mass too. No matter how hard Tsena kicked, Nooki could not pull his legs out of the muck. The more he struggled, the deeper he sank. He tossed his head and whinnied.

Tsena looked back, his heart pounding hard against his chest. The *tejanos* were upon them, firing their guns and yelling. He kicked the horse again and again, but it was no use. The horses were jammed together from all sides. Bullets whined through the air like wind through bare branches in the winter. He raised his arm and held the shield behind his back.

On his left a warrior jerked forward and fell onto Tsena's leg between their horses. Nooki whinnied, lurched up onto the horse ahead, and sank on his hind legs. Tsena looked around at the writhing confusion. He had to get out of this trap. Holding his shield, he jumped onto the back of the horse ahead of him and turned, stepping from one horse to the next toward the edge of the herd. He fell, but the horses were so close together that he could not fall to the ground.

Something slammed into the shield, knocking him down across the horses—a bullet surely. He scrambled up and kept going, holding Grandfather's shield between him and the *tejanos*. The air was filled with the crack of gunfire, whining bullets, screaming women and horses.

Out of breath, he reached the edge of the struggling mass and jumped down. He ran, keeping his shield behind him. Then up ahead he saw a red mare standing under the branches of a liveoak.

Brothers

"Yuaneh!" yelled Tsena.

The mare turned, swiveled her ears, and bolted toward him. He grabbed her tether on the run and flung himself on her back. For a moment he clung to her neck, riding at a tearing gallop across the prairie, her golden mane and the ribbons whipping across his face. She knew the way, Spirit Wolf said, and Tsena let her go. He could see other warriors riding for their lives—one and two on a horse or with women clinging to their waists.

Tsena raised his head and snatched a glance over his shoulder. Three *tejanos* were pursuing him! He crouched over Yuaneh again and clung like a burr. "Fly, fly!" he murmured in her ear.

Yuaneh raced on across the prairie, through a stand of trees, and out into the open again. Ahead lay a warrior sprawled on the ground. Tsena did not know whether he was wounded or dead. He only knew he could not pass him by.

He felt for the loop braided into her mane, slipped it over his head, and let himself down on her side. She galloped on, headed for the warrior. She knew what they had to do. Her hooves pounded the ground near Tsena's head, and he gripped so tightly with his legs and feet that he could feel her heart pounding.

The warrior rolled over and raised himself up on one arm, holding his side. It was Kiyou! Tsena reached out with both arms, and they grabbed hold of each other. The rope bit into his bare chest, and with one wrenching heave he swung Kiyou up and across Yuaneh. For a moment Tsena lay over him, gasping for breath as the little mare galloped on.

Kiyou stirred, straining until he was astride, and then collapsed over Yuaneh's neck. Her shoulders were pumping hard now, her head dipping with each stride. Foam flew from her muzzle, and Tsena knew she could not keep up this pace with two on her back. So what was he to do?

Shots split the air. He glanced over his shoulder. The *tejanos* had not gained on him, but they were still coming. He moved his shield arm to cover his back.

Far in the distance he saw a curving line of trees. A

creek. He had an idea—it was their only hope. He jabbed his heels into Yuaneh's sides.

"Fly, Yuaneh, fly like the wind!"

From somewhere deep inside, the mare found more strength. She spurted forward, leaving the *tejanos* farther and farther behind. Now great globs of foam flecked with blood flew from her muzzle as they galloped for the creek.

Tsena crouched over Kiyou. Suddenly, tree branches scraped his shield. Yuaneh splashed through the creek and tore through the underbrush. Tsena pressed his knee to her flank, and they swung sharply to the left for a short way. Then, nudging Yuaneh back into the creek, he headed in the opposite direction. It was an old trick, but it might fool the *tejanos*.

At a bend in the creek Tsena dismounted, led Yuaneh into the bushes, and stopped still. She raised her muzzle and drew great breaths through flaring nostrils. Kiyou lifted his head and looked at him with widened eyes. Tsena put his fingertips over his mouth for silence. His heart pounded as he listened for the *tejanos*. Would they follow the false trail? He heard them galloping closer, heard them yelling to each other. Then they splashed through the creek, and the sound of hooves faded in the distance.

Tsena had fooled them—this time anyway. Now he must find a better place to hide until dark because they might be back. No telling how many *tejanos* were out looking for *Nemena*. Yes, they would hide until dark and then ride for home.

He led Yuaneh along the creek bed while Kiyou sat holding his hand on the wound, his head slumped forward. Neither of them spoke. Occasionally, Tsena stopped and listened for the *tejanos*.

Father Sun had reached the zenith when Tsena found an embankment that hung over the creek—high enough to hide Yuaneh—and helped Kiyou down.

Kiyou did not look at him but sat on the sandy bank, leaning over and clutching his belly. "It feels like there is fire in my side."

Tsena knelt. "Let me look at it."

Kiyou took his hand away. Blood flowed from a small, jagged hole in the right side of his belly. Tsena knew it had to be stopped.

"Put your hand back," Tsena said. "It needs binding."

He crawled up a gully, peered over the top, and looked around without moving. After a time he crept noiselessly out to the meadow and pulled a handful of grass.

"Here, press this to it," he said when he returned to Kiyou. Then he cut a length of vine and tied it around Kiyou's waist to hold the grass in place.

With a groan Kiyou eased himself back on one arm, lay down, and clenched his eyes shut. Tsena watched him for a moment. At one time he would not have cared whether Kiyou lived or died. But now that he was wounded, now that his sneering mouth was twisted in pain, Tsena could not leave him to his fate and ride home—though it would be so much easier. And there was the fact that Kiyou had saved him from the buffalo, whether he meant to or not.

He thought of the *tejanos*. Would they follow the creek back in this direction? Remembering the footprints he had made, he broke off a leafy branch, went out to the meadow, and swept them away.

Then he sat down beside Kiyou. There was nothing to do now but listen and wait and try to understand all that had happened. Many *Nemena* had died—he knew that. Even women and children, shot or trampled in that horrible bog. Was Kianceta one of them? Would the *tejanos* pursue them all the way to the hills? With a sigh Tsena leaned against the sandy embankment. It seemed that the Great Spirit had turned his face from them again. Och, *if only they had not tried to take all those horses*, Tsena thought.

Kiyou raised his head, his eyes shining unnaturally. "I may have a bullet in me, but I left an arrow in one of them. His heart sleeps—I am sure of it." He lay back and closed his eyes. "I am sure of it."

The buzzing of cicadas rose and fell in the sweltering still air, and in spite of his worry, Tsena's eyes shut and he sank into sleep.

All at once the sound of horses' hooves awoke him. They were coming closer! He took out his bow and crawled up the gully to have a look. Through the foliage he saw the same three *tejanos* approaching. He nocked an arrow, aimed at the man in the lead, and pulled the bowstring back. If they decided to come down to the creek, he would kill them.

One of the men looked in his direction, and Tsena held his breath. The muscles in his bow arm quivered with the strain of keeping his arrow poised.

But the *tejano* looked away and the three rode on around a curve in the creek. Slowly he released the bowstring. His head felt light. He wanted to run and leap and fling his arms up to the sky. He had fooled them, he was safe, and now, as soon as dark came, he could start home! *They* could start home.

When he slid down the gully, Kiyou was sitting up, watching him.

"I saw that you would kill *tejanos* rather than . . . rather than leave me lying here."

Tsena nodded. "There was a time when I swore I would leave you lying where you fell. But then you saved my life on the hunt." He felt a smile spread across his face. "Just do not call me a woman again or I might change my mind."

Kiyou turned away. "There is something I want to say, but you do not make it easy."

Tsena waited, not moving.

Kiyou grimaced, either with the pain of the wound or the words he was about to utter.

"You saved my life back there. It is hard to admit, but I will not forget it—not even if I live for a hundred winters."

Tsena's mouth opened. He stood looking down at Kiyou, scarcely able to believe the words.

"It was my duty—you would have done the same," he managed and dropped to his knees. "Let me look at your wound again."

The grass was matted with dried blood and stuck to his side.

"It has stopped bleeding. Can you crawl to the creek?"

"I think so," Kiyou said. Grunting, he made his way on his hands and knees.

Tsena scooped up some water and washed the grass and dirt from the wound.

Kiyou lifted his face to the sky. "We lost many warriors," he said through clenched teeth.

Tsena nodded. "The women will be mourning for moons."

"But one day the *white* women will cry—you will see—when I take my uncle's place."

Tsena looked up at the sky. *Will we ever learn?* he wondered. But he said, "You need a poultice on your wound."

Not far from the creek he found a prickly pear, hacked the needles from a leaf, and peeled it.

When he had bound the juicy pad to Kiyou's side, he said, "So, that will draw the poison out."

"From my heart too, Brother," Kiyou said and looked away quickly.

Tsena nodded. "And from mine, Brother."

Before darkness fell, Tsena waded into the creek and washed the dust and sweat from his body. Then, opening his parfleche, he took out a strip of jerky, tore it into two pieces, and handed one to Kiyou.

Later that night when the moon rose and crickets sang *cree-cree, cree-cree*, they mounted and started for home. At last the terrible day had come to an end.

Lone Hill

Five sleeps passed as Tsena and Kiyou moved slowly toward home, traveling only by night until they reached the hills. Once a day Tsena changed Kiyou's dressing. Even though he had a bullet in his side, the wound was beginning to heal, and he grew stronger. Strong enough to ride behind Tsena now.

When the setting sun was only two fingers above the horizon, they came to Lone Hill. It cast a long shadow across the land, reaching out to touch them. Tsena reined in and sat gazing at the hill.

He remembered when he had first climbed the hill, his small hand clutched in Grandfather's big rough one. How he had to stretch his legs to step up the limestone ledges. Once Grandfather lifted him in the air and he squealed.

It was on this eastern slope that Ahsenap wished to be buried, in a rocky crevice facing the rising sun. Tsena knew that one day he would have to carry his grandfather's body up there and bury him. He could see those rocks now, forming a ledge about halfway up the hill.

"So, we are home," Kiyou said in a quiet voice.

Tsena only nodded. He pressed his heels to Yuaneh's side, and they rode on.

At the edge of the meadow they stopped and gazed at the village spread along the creek. The sound of women wailing rose and fell.

"Perhaps they mourn us too," Tsena said.

Beside the creek women and girls were filling their water bags. Chawakeh tied up her bag and stood, struggling to lift it. Then, as the dogs began to bark, she looked over and saw them. She dropped the bag and ran.

"Mother!" she yelled. "My brother has come—and Kiyou."

Yuaneh needed no signal to start toward the village. Women and girls ran to meet them and crowded around, singing the tremolo.

Kianceta appeared from among the lodges, and Tsena felt his heart leap. His friend was alive! Kianceta waved both arms over his head as he ran, yelling, "Tsena Naku!" again and again. "I thought . . ." he gasped as he stopped beside Yuaneh, "we thought . . ." He looked from one to the other.

Tsena jumped off and grasped Kianceta by the shoulders, grinning. "It makes my heart glad to see you alive, Ceta."

"Mine too, but there is much mourning." Looking at Kiyou, Kianceta said, "Even your uncle's wife and little Miakah . . ." He shook his head. "The women wail day and night."

"We heard them," Kiyou said, dismounting. "But one of my arrows pierced the heart of a *tejano* and stopped its crying."

An old warrior approached. He had many war pictures on his body. "Your wound is a mark of honor," he said.

Kiyou nodded his thanks. "It was Tsena Naku who saved my life."

The crowd made way as Topay and Ekakura, Kiyou's mother, came running. Their faces and arms were bloodied, their dresses torn.

Topay stopped before him. Her mouth opened, but for a moment no words came.

"My son," she said then, "you return! I made new moccasins in hopes they would bring you home. Come, I will get them, and you can rest while I prepare food."

"Yes, Mother, but first I must find Grandfather. Does he wait for me?"

"Yes, my son. He kept saying you would return."

The old man sat cross-legged under a brush arbor that stood beside his lodge. His right eyelid drooped, but his left eye shone. Tears ran down his wrinkled cheeks.

Tsena took the shield from his arm, removed his bowcase, and sat down before him.

"I knew you would return, Grandson. Your wolf medicine is strong."

"Your shield too, Grandfather."

"Yes, but we have lost many warriors—six including Isimanica." Then Ahsenap named them, counting on his crooked fingers. Five were seasoned warriors, and one was a novice only a winter older than Tsena. It was worse than he feared.

"My granddaughter tells me you rescued Kiyou," Ahsenap went on.

Tsena nodded.

"That makes my heart glad, for it is more honorable to save a brother than to kill the enemy. Tell me the story."

Presently Chawakeh, who had been watching them from the doorway of the lodge, ran to Ahsenap. The black puppy scampered along at her feet. She knelt beside the old man and waited until he turned and put a hand on her shoulder. Ona waited too, as if the dog understood the sanctity of old age.

"You wish something, my little prairie flower?"

"My mother says it is time for the evening meal."

He smiled. "Then tell her that we come."

When Tsena entered the lodge, Topay motioned him to the place of honor. She had washed the blood from her face and arms and treated the cuts with powdered herbs. She wore her white doeskin dress for the occasion.

Grandmother Semanaw nodded to Tsena. "Welcome home, son of my daughter," she said in her gruff voice.

"Thank you, Grandmother, it pleases me to see you."

It was nearly dark. With the lodge cover rolled up, the fire flickered, lighting the faces of the family gathered around. Tsena's heart swelled with the joy of being home.

Topay served buffalo meat roasted with honey. Before they began to eat, Ahsenap raised a morsel on high.

"To you, Great Spirit, I offer the first morsel in gratitude for the return of my beloved grandson." He buried it in the fire pit, and they began to eat.

Chawakeh stole glances at Tsena with her bright, black eyes. Ona sat at her side, his tail slowly sweeping back and forth, for the little girl always gave him a bite or two when no one was looking.

"Will you ask my brother to tell us a story, Grandfather? About the Great Water?"

"Hush, my daughter," Topay said. "Your brother is tired and hungry. He wishes only to eat now."

"No, Mother, I feel revived already," Tsena said. "Tell my sister the Great Water is like the prairie grass rippling in the wind—only it is the color of the sky.

Winged boats float on it and bring white men here from the land on the other side."

Chawakeh scowled. "Then maybe they will take them back."

"I wish it were so, little prairie flower," said Ahsenap, "but white man hungers for our land."

With her back as straight as an arrow, Semanaw said, "I do not wish to hear about white man."

"Whether you wish or not, my wife, you shall," said Ahsenap.

After the meal was over Chawakeh brought around a bowl of fresh water, and Tsena washed his fingers. Ahsenap arose with a grunt and motioned him to come.

"Bring fire, Grandson. We will smoke the pipe."

Tsena picked up a lighted stick and followed the old man out into the night. They walked along the creek away from the village and sat on a rock ledge. From a distance the lodges glowed with firelight.

Ahsenap took out his pipe, pressed tobacco in the bowl, and handed it to Tsena. "My pipe is yours now."

Tsena caught his breath. "Mine, Grandfather?"

"Yes, you are worthy of it."

Tsena gave the fire stick to Ahsenap and cradled the pipe in both hands. "To you, Great Spirit," he said raising it to the sky. As he put the stem to his lips Grandfather touched fire to the bowl, and Tsena filled his body with the sacred smoke.

They smoked together in silence until the pipe was

finished. Then Tsena cleaned it and put it back in the case.

At last Ahsenap said, "Kianceta tells me you rode at Pochana Quoheep's side."

"Yes, Grandfather."

"Tell me, why did he allow the war party to be so burdened down?"

Tsena drew a deep breath. "He did not approve of taking all that loot, Grandfather, but many of the warriors, including Isimanica, wanted it." He pulled the book from his sash. "I took something too—a book of ancient words, three thousand winters old."

Ahsenap only nodded. He did not reach out his hand for the book. "More and more our people want what white man has," he said. "They would even die for it."

The two sat listening to the warble of tree frogs. Tsena knew that his grandfather had not finished.

"And white man wants what we have. He wants our hunting grounds, and he will die for it. In the end he will take it, and we will have to walk his road." He paused. "Of course, I will be in the land beyond by then."

Grandfather put his hand on Tsena's knee. "But I know that the same blood that creeps like the snail in my body, leaps like a torrent in yours." He straightened his back, and looked up into the starry sky. "Someday you will be chief like your father, so you must not marry early. You must wait until you have acquired many horses of your own to give for a highborn girl."

Tsena felt the blood rise to his face as he thought of Anawakeo.

"There is a girl in your heart?" Ahsenap asked.

Tsena gasped. "How can you know everything, Grandfather? Did my mother tell you?"

"No." He was silent for a moment. "May I hear her name?"

"You will not tell anyone—not even Grandmother?"

"It will be our secret, Grandson."

"Anawakeo," he blurted out, "granddaughter of the great chief."

"Ah–h–h–h. You could not have chosen better. And does she return your feeling?"

"Yes."

"She will require many horses."

"I will get them, Grandfather."

The old man gazed up at the stars. For a long time neither of them spoke. They listened to the breeze soughing in the liveoak trees that grew along the creek.

"You know white man's heart better than any of us," Ahsenap said then. "It is you who must treat with him. Learn to read his signs, Grandson. But also show him how to read the signs of the earth and sky."

The waning moon rose, and Ahsenap stirred himself. "I say good night now. My limbs grow weary under the weight of sixty-four winters."

Tsena helped him up. "Grandfather, I will hold your words in my heart."

Nodding, he took Tsena's hand in his rough ones and patted it. Then he turned and shuffled off in the darkness.

As Tsena stood there alone, a wolf howled from the direction of Lone Hill. He mounted Yuaneh and rode through the dark to the bottom of the hill. It loomed large and black, but he could have climbed it with his eyes closed. He knew every ledge, every tree, every creature's den. He dismounted and left Yuaneh to graze.

At the top he heard the wolf again—this time very near. A thrill went through him. Though he did not see Spirit Wolf, he felt his presence. He raised his arms and sang.

> "*The white wolves come running,*
> *The white wolves come running.*
> *Behold them and listen,*
> *Behold them and speak.*"

Suddenly, Tsena understood his vision song. The white wolves were white men and he must listen and speak to them. Grandfather knew it too.

He gazed at the dark vastness of the earth below. He sensed the life that slept upon it or hunted in the night. The rising moon seemed to hold Spirit Wolf in its light. Even though Tsena stood on Lone Hill, he was not alone.

Glossary

COMANCHE WORDS

ahey	I claim it
mariah weh	good morning
Nemena	the People
och!	oh!
puha	medicine, power
puhakut	medicine man

SPANISH WORDS

adelante (ah–deh–LAHN–tay)	forward
adios (ah–dee–OSE)	farewell
ahora (ah–OR–ah)	now
Alemán (ah–leh–MAN)	German
bueno (BWEH–no)	good
casa (CAH–sah)	house
casita (cah–SEE–tah)	little house
claro (CLAH–roh)	of course
comprende (cohm–PREN–deh)	you understand
de nada (deh NAH–dah)	you're welcome
desayuno (deh–say–YOO–no)	breakfast
día (DEE–ah)	day

gracias (GRAH–see–us)	thanks
hasta luego (AHS–tah loo–EH–go)	until then
hermosa (ehr–MOSE–ah)	beautiful
hola (OH-lah)	hello
iglesia (ig–LAY–see–uh)	church
más (mahs)	more
masa de maíz (MAH-sah deh mah-EES)	corn mush
mexicano (meh–hee–CAH–no)	Mexican
momento (moh–MEN–toh)	moment
muchacho (moo–CHA–cho)	boy
mucho (MOO–cho)	much
muy (MOO–ey)	very
nada (NAH–dah)	nothing
otra vez (OH–trah vehz)	again
perro (PEHR–roh)	dog
por favor (pohr fah–VOR)	please
qué lástima (kay LAHS-teem-ah)	what a pity
quizás (kee–SAHS)	perhaps
seda (SEH–dah)	silk
señor (seen–YOR)	mister
señora (seen–YOR–ah)	mistress
sí (see)	yes
tejano (teh–HAH–no)	Texan
tocar (toh–CAR)	to touch
tres (trace)	three
un (oon)	one
vamonos (VAH–moh–nos)	let's go
verdad (vehr–DAHD)	true

About the Author

JANICE SHEFELMAN is the daughter of a German professor and his wife, and grew up in a university neighborhood in Dallas, Texas. Her father read to her from an early age, which began a love affair with books and led to careers as teacher, librarian, and writer. Books opened the door to a big world and gave her the desire to see it. Even though Mrs. Shefelman has traveled all around the world, she loves to write about Texas, especially its past.

"I am fascinated with bringing the past to life," she explained. "When we found arrowheads on my family's ranch, I began to wonder about the people who had once lived there. What were their lives like? What were their hopes and dreams? So I read all the books I could find and, in the process, fell in love with the Comanches."

Mrs. Shefelman's books have received many honors: *A Paradise Called Texas* is a Texas Bluebonnet Award Nominee, and *A Peddler's Dream* is a Reading Rainbow Book, NCSS/CBC Notable Book, and an *American Bookseller* "Pick of the Lists."

She lives in Austin, Texas, with her husband, Tom, who is also her illustrator and an architect. For more information visit their website at Shefelmanbooks.com.